The Value of Everything and Nothing
Karen Friedlander

Marbrook Publishing - Madison, WI
ISBN: 978-0-692-19782-0
The Value of Everything and Nothing | Karen Friedlander
Available formats: eBook
Paperback distribution

Other books by this Karen Friedlander:

A Person of Value
A Valuable Life
A Valuable Lesson

The Value of Everything and Nothing

Prologue

Maryland Senator Jarod Abrams was irate and seething. He sincerely hoped that his anti-hypertensive medication would kick in if his systolic blood pressure passed the point of no return and a stroke was imminent. At this moment, the angry man really wanted to kill another person. He truly believed that he could do the deed himself if he had any idea where to find Michael Anderson or Michael Wyatt, or whatever the hell the bastard was calling himself nowadays!

Part One
Chapter One

Jarod Abrams, the very distinguished senator representing the small Mid-Atlantic state in Congress, had led a charmed life of privilege from the day that he had been born to quite wealthy Jewish parents in the suburbs of Baltimore. As an only son, he was spoiled and entitled from the moment he left the crib. He was sent to all the "right" primary and secondary schools, and then he was trundled off to Yale, his father's alma mater. He studied law and eventually earned a prestigious degree from that august and respected institution.

After graduation, there had been numerous offers to join local law firms, but Jarod had other aspirations. It wasn't until he had tediously worked his way through the criminal justice system to become Maryland's State's Attorney General that he took a break from the courtroom. There was a motive behind that unexpected choice. Mr. Abrams wanted to make himself available for appointment to a federal judgeship if it came his way. Perhaps, that was the first disenchanted moment in his empowered life. That coveted position was never offered, so a disgruntled man had to set his cap for something else. Finally, he settled for being part of a federal body in Washington DC that legislated the law rather than interpreted it when he ran for a seat in the United States Congress.

Abrams had all the right connections and the right image to make that a quick reality. With very little actual campaigning, he easily won the Democratic nomination and steamrolled over his Republican opponent. He was a shoo-in whenever each new election rolled around, and was as much of a fixture as Senator Barbara Mikulski had been for thirty years. He currently divided his time between Washington and his Tudor mansion in bucolic and pricey northwest Baltimore County. Although now older, he was still a very handsome man with piercing blue eyes and a head of thick dark hair, and he still had the same attractive woman by his side that he had married decades ago. She had borne him two perfect sons, Jason and Justin. Those boys proudly represented the third generation of Abrams males to attend Yale.

Everything had been copacetic in his storybook life except for one small hiccup that occurred when he had been a cocky and impetuous eighteen-year-old. He had a brief and unwise dalliance with a young and giddy teenage girl who became pregnant with his child. Perhaps that airhead thought that she could trap him into making her his wife. After all, she seemed as infatuated with his wealth and station in life as she was with him. However, he quickly set her straight. She wasn't from either his social strata or even his religion, and he had college plans in the works that would begin the following fall. He was going places, and he didn't need some albatross slung around his neck.

Jennifer Anderson, the silly erstwhile paramour, finally got the message and Jarod assumed that she had slunk off to have an abortion at some welfare clinic in the city. It simply wasn't his problem to solve. However, it all came back to bite him in the ass. It wasn't until years later that he found out there had been no termination of the unwelcome pregnancy. Although this abandoned girl would later die on the streets from a crack addiction, she had first left a part of herself and him behind. Eventually, he would come face to face with the adult version of his illegitimate son, and that shocking first born's name had been changed to Michael Wyatt.

Michael Wyatt was just as conniving and opportunistic as his dead mother. He easily provided Jarod, then an attorney in private practice, with irrefutable concrete DNA evidence to prove paternity. Abrams used his own discrete lab to check the authenticity of the results, and any doubts vanished as mitochondria and alleles were perfectly aligned. Therefore, Wyatt was literally calling the shots, and, loaded with that ammunition, had blackmailed Abrams into representing him in court during a lengthy trial for a litany of federal crimes. It was ironic, really, since just months before, Abrams, in his role as Maryland's State's Attorney General, had been trying to nail the young upstart for those very same crimes.

Jarod Abrams was very good in the role of defense lawyer, so he eventually managed to get his client exonerated of all charges. Wyatt had looked smug rather than grateful when that transpired, and both men parted ways after the verdict had been read aloud. They were supposed to stay parted forever because Abrams was sure that his paternal debt had now been paid in full. The last words between them in the courtroom were menacing and quite succinct. Each man made it obvious that any connection that they shared, genetically or otherwise, was forever severed.

It took many months before Abrams let himself believe that Michael Wyatt intended to uphold their bargain. The young criminal had disappeared like a wisp of smoke soon after the trial, and apparently nobody seemed to know where he had gone. Now the son of a bitch was back and determined to ruin his biological father and cause upheaval in the Abrams family.

3

Chapter Two

Abrams was first made aware of Michael Wyatt's unwelcome return to his life in a circuitous way. His oldest boy, Jason, was finishing a stellar performance at Yale's Law School in New Haven, Connecticut. Currently, he was zealously being romanced by some very prestigious firms on Wall Street in nearby New York City. Those firms represented the rarefied echelons of corporate law where clients or companies didn't hesitate to fork over exorbitant $50,000 an hour fees. It didn't get any more exclusive than that, and a proud father couldn't have been more delighted with his offspring.

Senator Abrams was also just as pleased with Justin, Jason's younger brother, who was only a few years behind on a similar career path. Both of his "legitimate" sons were on an upward trajectory that was legal in every sense of the word. Now the "criminal" was back with an agenda that threatened to upset the whole applecart.

Jason had recently telephoned during one of the frequent congressional recesses and asked if his father could come to Connecticut for a brief discussion that was best to have in person. This was an unusual request because each of Jarod's sons were somewhat insular. Both dispassionately desired to make it on their own, and having their old man, the Senator, hovering around was equally an embarrassment as well as an invitation for gossip. Some jealous fellow students might try to make a case that the boys were using their father's clout to get ahead. Abrams was well aware of cutthroat tactics like that in those upscale private institutions. Of course, it frequently happened, but it was all done very discreetly.

4

The following day, Abrams' driver wended his way up the I-95 corridor to New Haven, and considerately waited in the limo while the Senator entered a nondescript rendition of a 1950s diner located far from the college campus. He was quite surprised to see both of his sons hunkered down in a back-booth nursing mugs of coffee and looking very serious.

"What's going on, guys?" Abrams asked curiously as he sat across from them. "Are you too embarrassed to be seen with your old man and that's why we're meeting here in a greasy spoon? We're probably running the risk of getting ptomaine poisoning if we eat the food."

"Yeah, maybe we are embarrassed to be seen with you, Dad," Jason responded boldly. "And we're not here to eat. There are some things that you need to read in private away from any prying eyes."

Almost simultaneously, both of Abrams' sons pulled folded pieces of paper from inside their jackets and laid them before him. It didn't take the Congressman long to figure out that they were two printout copies of emails sent to both Jason and Justin's personal college IP addresses. He quickly read the one meant for Jason.

"Hey there, Jason, or shall I say, Mr. Yale Law School Superstar! I've been keeping track of you over the years and am fairly sure that your father is one proud puppy right now. How could he not be busting the buttons on his three-piece suit when his heir-apparent is destined to join the glorified ranks of the rich and privileged upon graduation?

Well, my young dude, I hate to burst your little bubble of entitled complacency, but you ain't the next in line to the throne. No, sir! You're just like poor Prince Harry—not the primary heir but rather the 'spare.' I am the legitimate, or shall I say, 'illegitimate' usurper to that lofty position in the hierarchy because I was born first, long before you were even a lecherous leer in your father's eye. Now, let me reassure you that dear old Dad didn't defile your mother back in those early days. At least I'll grant him that tiny particle of dignity. However, he did defile and degrade my mother after his callous little fling. So, I just wanted you to know that your old man isn't some paragon of virtue, no matter what he claims. Just be sure to tell him that 'Michael,' your half-brother, sends his fondest regards."

Justin's email followed the same chatty, snide format, and it also contained the same explicit damning accusation asserting that Jarod had gotten a young woman pregnant long before he had ever met the mother of his current children. There weren't any overt intimidating threats, or anything spelled out that could be remotely construed as dangerous. However, Jarod knew that an implied warning was really being sent to him via his sons:

"I know who and what you are, Congressman Abrams, and what you did a long time ago. So beware the consequences of your callous actions of the past."

Chapter Three

Abrams tried to tough it out and opted for a cynically cavalier response.

"Are these stupid notes what has both of you looking like someone just spit in your soup? Get a grip, boys! Slanderous stuff like this happens all the time when you're a very public figure."

"It's only considered 'slander,' Dad, if the statements are blatantly false and meant to injure someone's reputation with untrue accusations," his oldest son informed him solemnly.

"You can't honestly believe this crap coming from someone who apparently is too cowardly to even sign his full fucking name!" Abrams sputtered.

"It's not that hard to believe," Justin chimed in. "Jason and I aren't stupid, and over the years we knew about all the little flings with secretaries, paralegals, and other young attorneys. We watched Mom cry each time someone would 'accidentally' let innuendo of your indiscretion slip. We can only assume that your current conquests have probably now been bumped up a notch to White House aides and staffers."

Abrams tried to sound outraged.

"That's simply ridiculous. Why have you allowed yourself to become jaded by some unfounded, malicious gossip that is probably coming from a disgusting, vindictive person?"

"Just exactly how many were there over the years?" Jason now wanted to know, ignoring his father's pitiful attempts to discredit the facts. "How many times did you cheat on Mom?"

"If I ever did hurt your mother—and I'm not saying that I did—that is a discussion that I should be having with her, not you," Abrams hissed forcefully. "If she is still married to me, doesn't that say something about the validity of what you claimed happened or is happening now?"

"Spoken like a true lawyer," Justin sniped. "Just what did you expect Mom to do? She was a sheltered young graduate of Sarah Lawrence with a liberal arts degree. She was never expected to use it. Her generation was supposed to marry the right prospect and make a home in the suburbs while looking presentable at cocktail parties. If she had tried to divorce you, her life would have become a living hell. So, you were pretty confident that she wouldn't rock the boat, and you simply went on your merry philandering way and paid for a lot of abortions. I guess you must have missed one, Dad."

"You two are being judgmental and ridiculous, and I can't believe that we're actually having this discussion," Abrams roared. "Just ignore these fucking emails unless they evolve into a blackmail attempt, and then I'll take steps to find out who this person is and nip it in the bud."

"This person's name is *Michael*," Justin said softly. "Ring any bells for you?"

"No, nor should it," Abrams lied.

"Well, Justin and I are putting you on notice, Dad. If this 'Michael' initiates contact with either of us, we're going to push for a face-to-face meeting and hear what he has to say," Jason vowed.

Abrams scowled but didn't respond. Any potential future meetings with Jason and Justin were never going to take place if he had anything to say about it. He surmised that Michael Wyatt really didn't want to meet his brothers. That was all smoke and mirrors to make an unrepentant father sweat. No, that scum had other ideas that were aimed at him personally. Wyatt had just initiated the first shot across his biological parent's bow—an omen of ugly things to come. An angry and very vengeful senator would find Michael Wyatt first and make him rue the day that he had ever poked his head up above the ground again.

An indignant father left his equally indignant sons in the diner and returned to his limo. His driver assumed that they would be returning to the bachelor apartment that the Senator maintained in Washington. However, he was told that there would be a temporary side trip to Baltimore. Surprisingly, the destination wasn't going to be the congressman's home in suburbia, but rather an old venerable law office located near the Inner Harbor in the city.

Chapter Four

Manus Kirchner was getting on in age. His name was still on the door of the law office denoting his importance as senior partner of the rather large firm of prestigious attorneys and associates, but it was really just a respectful formality. Manus' younger, long-time law partner, Ellis Faraday, really ran the firm, and was very good at keeping it healthy and prosperous even in times of recession and stock market upheavals. Manus still came in a few days a week, however, to keep his fingers in the pie. Or perhaps that was because his long-suffering wife wanted him out of the house when she had her canasta or mahjong gaggle of lady friends over. Today was one of those days that found him sitting behind his large mahogany desk like a wise Buddha as he perused some merger documents for a client.

Manus looked up over his half-glasses as a pretty, young secretary poked her head in the door with a stricken look on her face.

"Sir, there is a person here demanding to see you right now. It's Senator Jarod Abrams. He doesn't have an appointment penciled in on my calendar, so perhaps you may have made one on your personal electronic scheduler. Shall I show him in?"

"Well, by all means, appointment or not, please show the distinguished Congressman into my humble abode," Manus replied cynically. "We mustn't leave his eminence hanging about at loose ends."

"I heard that, you washed-up and broken old has-been," Abrams sneered as he rudely pushed past the young woman.

The girl was flustered but managed to ask timidly, "Would you like some water, coffee, or tea, Sir?"

"Just get the hell out already," Abrams yelled, "and make sure to close the damn door behind you!"

Manus sat back and studied the belligerent man before him.

"Well, you certainly still like to make a grand and haughty entrance, Jarod, and your manners haven't improved one iota over time. So, tell me, to what do I owe the honor of your irritating presence today?"

"We need to talk about Michael Wyatt," Abrams said as he paced the room. "I need to get in touch with him, and you're going to tell me where he is."

"Am I?" Manus asked innocently.

"He was your client the last time I checked, so you must have some idea where he is now," Abrams insisted.

Manus raised his eyebrows as he responded.

"I may be getting old, but I'm not senile yet, Jarod, because I distinctly remember that *you* were the last person to see him in your capacity as the defending attorney who represented him in court. You argued his case against all those trumped up federal charges, and you were the one who triumphed in that endeavor. So, hats off to your slickness, Jarod. Ergo, Mr. Wyatt was *your* client the last time that anyone ever saw the lad again. If you've lost track of him, that's on you. If he owed you money, you may as well just write it off as a financial loss and quit crying about it."

"Don't try to get all coy with me, Manus," Abrams sneered. "You and Wyatt were as thick as thieves back in the day. Philip Symington taught him well, and he was guilty of each and every one of those federal crimes listed on the indictment. You probably knew it, and maybe you were even complicit in some of them."

Manus' stare was hard.

"Be very careful regarding those accusations, Jarod, because they are a two-edged sword. One could argue that you were just as guilty of malfeasance because you were instrumental in getting him acquitted."

"Everything was above board and legal," Abrams snapped. "Even though I knew that he was guilty as sin, a lawyer's job is to make sure that his client gets a fair and just defense according to the law. That's *all* that I did. I didn't levy the verdict; a jury of his peers decided to turn him loose, so that's not on me."

"And now it seems as if you've managed to misplace him," Manus smirked. "Want to tell me what has come up that is suddenly so urgent?"

"That's none of your business, you old fool," Abrams said forcefully.

Manus sat back and narrowed his eyes so that he almost looked reptilian. He had used that glare many times in the past to make witnesses sweat when they were on the hot seat testifying in court.

"I've known you since you were a little snot in short pants, Jarod. Back then you were very arrogant, but you were also sly and devious like a weasel. You always had an agenda, and no tactic was too low or despicable if it got you what you wanted. Well, guess what, this time you're not getting the prize. Even if I knew where Michael is, I wouldn't tell you because you definitely mean him harm in some fashion."

Abrams bent over the wide desk and got into the lawyer's personal space as he threatened menacingly, "I can be a very formidable enemy, Manus, so you may want to rethink your position. I can make your life hell by turning over some rocks. Maybe I'll start with 'The Haven.' Aren't you chairman of the board for that gussied-up orphanage out in Westminster? Perhaps I'll have a forensic accountant go over your books to see where the funds come from to keep it afloat. I have the clout to make that happen in a heartbeat with just the right amount of leverage."

"Knock yourself out, Jarod," Manus responded in a cool tone of voice bordering on icy. "There's nothing going on of an improper nature, and we welcome anyone's perusal of our finances. You'll just end up with lots of egg on your face, sonny boy."

"We'll just see about that," Abrams hissed as he made his exit.

After the door had slammed, Manus sat back and steepled his fingers in front of his lips. It was his go-to deep thinking posture. Somehow, this whole little drama today seemed to be the harbinger of an urgent, convoluted manhunt for some reason. But what was the connection between the two men?

Manus had always wondered how it had come about that Michael had managed to get Abrams to represent him in court. The year before that all went down, the State's Attorney had been trying to nail the young man's ass to the wall. Why the sudden about face? At the time, there seemed to be a whole subplot to this curious conundrum, but Manus was wise enough never to ask about the details. Actually, he had never been afforded the opportunity to pry because, not long after that infamous trial, Michael had simply vanished from Baltimore.

Even though Manus never saw Michael Wyatt in person again, there had been much detailed long-distance contact. After his mysterious disappearance, correspondence via the Internet enabled construction of "The Haven," thanks to some very generous funds rerouted from Michael's untraceable off-shore accounts in the Caymans.

The wise old attorney still remained ignorant of Michael's whereabouts or why he had fled over a decade and a half ago.

Wherever he was now, Manus fervently hoped that he would stay off the grid and out of Abrams' crosshairs. That odious political prick was trouble!

Chapter Five

Jarod Abrams was livid as the chauffeur left Baltimore's Inner Harbor and accessed Interstate 95 that would take them to Washington. The irate Senator was racking his brain for other avenues that he could use to locate Wyatt. It was imperative that he stop him in his tracks before "whatever'" escalated and became an inferno that Jarod couldn't easily put out. He continued to be distracted when he reached his apartment in the District of Columbia, and the funk lasted late into the night causing his latest fling to depart in a pout when he couldn't perform.

At some point during those long dark hours, his mind glommed onto a flimsy straw. Back in the day when he had been investigating Wyatt for racketeering, fraud, theft, income tax evasion, and everything else that he could throw into the mix, he had turned to the Feds for assistance. He remembered one particular Special Agent in charge of the Baltimore FBI field office named David Parrish. Jarod had even asked the perceptive G-Man to sit in on the initial interrogation when the witch hunt had just begun.

Back then, Parrish had a reputation as a go-getter, and he was said to hang on like a stubborn terrier when he had just the smallest hint of something hinky. Maybe the guy had kept his old notes even after the case went nowhere, or maybe he continued to keep an eagle-eye peeled for something down the road. Abrams knew that it was worth a shot to ask, but he wanted to keep this on the down low. He'd have to finesse his approach to Parrish so that the federal agent wouldn't begin to wonder why Abrams was suddenly rehashing yesterday's old news. The politico made a snap decision. He would drive himself to Baltimore the next day.

The Senator still maintained useful contacts in Baltimore, and found out that Parrish had left the FBI several years ago and transferred to the Department of Justice in Washington DC. However, that was a short-lived upscale move because it wasn't very long before the former agent had taken early retirement and returned to his hometown. It certainly wasn't hard to find an address for him in a condominium down near the Harbor.

~~~~~~~~~

David Parrish had taken a page out of Michael's playbook and had reinvented himself after retiring from government service. It was an inevitable reaction given the last case that he had investigated. That digging had resulted in two innocent deaths and almost the forfeiture of his own life when a government conspiracy was uncloaked at the highest level. Michael had been literally right by David's side at the time, and his quick assistance was the only thing that saved David's life one night. Michael had spirited the older man away in the nick of time and stashed him in a safe house to recuperate from a deep shoulder wound.

Somehow, while David was down for the count, Michael and his friend, Sam Spade, had managed to foil a sinister and Machiavellian government plot, and thus remove the danger-filled bull's eye from David's back. However, the seeds of distrust regarding "the system" had already been sown, and the disgruntled former FBI agent wanted out.

Like a homing pigeon, he had returned to Baltimore with a few boxes of household paraphernalia and his adopted stray cat, and set up house with Bunny, a saucy little redhead who played the cello in the Baltimore Symphony Orchestra. Even though she was twenty years his junior, she seemed to adore him, and, after an eternity of lonely, divorced years, David tied the knot once more.

The mismatched couple couldn't have been happier, and now David spent his time hunting and pecking on his laptop as he churned out fictional novels that readers seemed to enjoy. His previous two attempts, *The Hollow Soul* and *The Mockery*, were thinly veiled allusions to rather serpentine government conspiracies, and David's fans ate it up and clamored for more. Now he was tediously creating his next book entitled, *A Pact with the Devil*.

Readers asked him all the time at book signings where he found his inspiration, and he would just smile and say that his brain was like a dark maze of disjointed ideas that somehow coalesced on the written page. In reality, Sam Spade, Michael's friend and a disavowed former CIA operative, was a fount of information. Although Sam never named names, he told tale after tale that would have had Ripley's "Believe It or Not" turning a skeptical eye. It certainly was good fodder for best-selling books.

It wasn't as if David and Sam were close. The only reason that they even knew each other was because of Michael. Early on, David had realized that the private investigator operated on a different stratum, and that playing field was not always legal. David wasn't sure that "Sam Spade" was even the guy's real name. For a time, the quirky question mark had flirted with the new alias of "Jay Silverheels," but that hadn't lasted long. Perhaps the "Sam Spade" persona was his only real comfort zone.

As for David's relationship with Michael—well, that was a mixed bag of emotional ties.

Chapter Six

David had known Michael since he had been an unfettered wild child on the rough streets of Baltimore. At the time, David had felt pity for the little waif, but he was so mired down in his own daughter's fatal illness and the disintegration of his stressed marriage that he had done absolutely nothing to improve the boy's sorry lot in life. Nevertheless, the kid had somehow attached himself to David as the distraught man descended into his own tortured hell, and, ultimately, a young throwaway kid showed more compassion than a grieving father was capable of exhibiting.

Fast-forward many years to their next encounter and its sentiment—one of mutual distrust. Suddenly, an adult version of that boy was going by the name of Michael Wyatt and residing with an older scion of Baltimore society. That generous patron would pass away, but a young protégé had learned how to make his way in the criminal world, and he was very good at it. However, a bond had been resurrected, and it was hard to put a label on it—perhaps a shared respect for the other's talents. To make a long story short, Michael tacitly helped David, now an FBI agent, to solve crimes. And that made David a superstar at the Bureau.

Undoubtedly, debts had been accrued, and a compromised FBI agent had repaid his by helping to cover up Michael's crime in a Cape Cod beach house. Much later, the young man would then make good on what he owed by saving David's life on a Baltimore street. Maybe it was Fate that had a hand in shaping their strange tenuous relationship. Maybe the two men had been around the block a time or two in another life.

Whatever the case, they seemed to be karmically tied together as they moved through this one. On David's end, he now felt a fondness for the man who had become a law-abiding architect on the west coast. That person was also a devoted husband and father who currently went by the new name of "Michael Devereaux." David liked to think that perhaps Michael had developed a soft spot for him as well.

In the late morning, David was fleshing out his notes for *A Pact with the Devil* when he was suddenly interrupted in the development of his convoluted plotline by the doorbell to the condominium. Bunny was away at the symphony hall for a rehearsal, so David and his cat padded over to answer the door. The distracted author was perplexed to find a familiar face staring back at him. Perhaps familiar wasn't an accurate word. Even though the two men had once shared a brief past encounter, there hadn't been any follow-up, nor had they established a working relationship in any sense of the word. The man standing outside in the hall was familiar to David simply because the politician had been representing the state of Maryland in the Senate for years.

Jarod Abrams afforded David a slight smile and asked if he could perhaps have a few minutes of his time to discuss a small matter. David opened the door wider and showed the Senator to the living room where he took a seat in a club chair.

"Well, this is certainly a surprise, Senator," David admitted. "What did you want to discuss with me?"

The Senator didn't answer right away. He was busy taking in his surroundings as if he were evaluating the cost of the draperies and the furniture. When he noted the laptop and the messy stack of papers on the dining table, he smiled in what David could only interpret as a condescending smirk.

"I've been told that you opted out of the government sector and decided to become an author of sorts. How's that going for you?"

"It's going well, thank you," David softly answered in an even tone.

"That odd new career choice really surprises me," Abrams goaded. "You were such a gung-ho FBI agent back in the day, but then I suppose that we all tend to slow down a bit as we get older. At least a little hobby can keep your brain cells firing on all cylinders."

"Yes, I'm staving off dementia by doing something that I love," David said through clenched teeth as he then lobbed his own veiled insult. "It seemed that while being employed in Washington DC, I came to the sad conclusion that government service is not always what it's cracked up to be by any stretch of the imagination. Some might even say that it's almost duplicitous."

Not to be outdone, Abrams quickly retorted, "Well, just be very careful what you write in your quaint little novels. You wouldn't want to be sued for libel."

David was tired of sniping. "I'm sure that you made the trip back to Baltimore and to my doorstep for a reason. Exactly what did you want to discuss with me, Senator Abrams?"

"Michael Wyatt!" was the unexpected response.

Chapter Seven

David was certainly not prepared for that curt answer, but he adroitly forced his expression to show bewilderment.

"Well, that takes me back quite a ways," he said slowly. "If my failing memory serves me, perhaps it was at least fifteen or so years ago. Maybe you can refresh my memory."

Abrams' expression was suddenly very serious. "When I was the State's Attorney General, we were investigating the Mob's presence in the city. Wyatt became a person of interest because, at that point, he had inherited Philip Symington's business enterprise and we were trying to make a connection. I asked the FBI for assistance in tying him to the interstate trafficking of stolen goods."

"Oh, right, right!" David said as if the light had gone on in his attic. "But if I remember correctly, that was an uphill battle at the time and took quite a while. However, now that you've brought up the subject, perhaps you would be good enough to explain something that puzzled me at the time. When a boatload of indictments were finally handed down against Michael Wyatt, weren't you a private attorney at that juncture and then represented him at his trial? I believe that you even got him off. That seemed really out of character for someone who, initially, was so committed to proving him guilty."

Abrams shrugged lazily. "I'm afraid that was a very serious lapse in judgment, Mr. Parrish. I was taken in by his youth and his claims of innocence. It doesn't happen often, but I was quite wrong. Wyatt was as guilty of all those charges as the day is long, and I regret that my legal expertise left him on the street."

"But didn't he disappear from the 'street' not long after that trial?" David asked casually. "The FBI certainly could never find a trace of where he went."

"Well, wherever he went, he's back now," Abrams informed David. A leopard can't change its spots, and he's into some troubling business that I want to stop permanently before it takes on a life of its own. I'm not sure where he is physically, so that presents a problem for me and I'll need some help locating his whereabouts," Abrams said earnestly. After a slight pause, he continued.

"What is of paramount importance is keeping the spotlight off of any digging that is done, and, likewise, my interest or involvement. I can't stress that enough. So, I was hoping that you may still have some old friends at the Baltimore branch of the FBI who could do some quiet, off the record investigating. Then you could pass that information along to me. I would be very appreciative if that happened, and I can certainly show my gratitude in many different ways."

David face took on a crestfallen expression. "I'm really very sorry, Senator Abrams, but I think that I may have burned all of my bridges at the Bureau a long time ago. And, just let me add one random observation. Your last comment reeks of being a bribe. I'm sure that I'm misconstruing your intent, but you may want to be careful how you phrase things. I would think that a savvy politician such as yourself would have more practice being circumspect."

Abrams' eyes narrowed as he abruptly stood up.

"Obviously, this was a colossal waste of my valuable time, Mr. Parrish, so I'll be going now," he said nastily as he made his way to the door.

"Stop back anytime, Senator, if you feel the need for more warm, heartfelt hospitality," David managed to get in the last word as he and the curious cat ushered their guest out of the condominium.

After the door had closed on the odious senator, David didn't return to his laptop. Instead, he plopped down on the sofa and began thinking about Michael Wyatt, who was now Michael Devereaux. David's orange tabby jumped into his lap and began purring contentedly while David mused about the new implications coming out of the blue.

"You could have been a bit more help, you know," David said softly to the feline as he stroked its soft ears. "You could have rubbed against the trouser legs of that clown's thousand-dollar suit so that he looked like he had an up close and personal encounter with a Wookie and lost the battle."

The cat completely ignored his owner's soulful complaint and began to fastidiously groom itself. Now, David was also wondering where Michael might be at the moment. It wasn't like they kept tabs on each other or exchanged Christmas cards. They led completely separate lives over 3,000 miles apart. David was in semi-retirement in Baltimore, and Michael was a busy and successful architect in San Francisco. He also had a wife and a family. To David's knowledge, Michael was leading the American dream sans anything illegal. So, what exactly had old Jarod Abrams' knickers in a twist? What had Michael done now? It was over five years since they had been in contact, so that gave David pause because Michael could be impulsive and unpredictable if he was threatened.

David decided that he didn't like unanswered questions, so he pulled out his cell phone and made a quick call.

"What's up, Ernest Hemingway? Did you suddenly develop writer's block?" Sam Spade's voice boomed in his ear.

"I need to have a face-to-face with you, Sam. When can you stop over?" David wanted to know.

"That certainly sounds mysterious," Sam Spade replied.

"Yeah, well, I am a mystery writer, you know. Maybe I'm just staying in character so that I don't disappoint you," David retorted.

"Okay, Buddy, you've managed to pique my curious side," Sam laughed. "I'll be over in a few."

When Sam Spade later arrived at the condominium, David got right to the point.

"Where is Michael and what is he up to?"

By now, Sam was used to David's impatient, in-your-face habit of getting right to the point with no finessing buildup. The man always wanted to know what he wanted to know, so he expected an immediate answer.

"Well now, care to tell me why the sudden interest in our mutual acquaintance?" Sam asked innocently.

"Don't pussyfoot around, Sam," David insisted. "You and Michael go back a long way, and you always turn to each other for help when there's a problem. Apparently, there is a problem now, and you're the one person that he would trust to help him."

"That's true," Sam agreed, "we always have each other's backs and do whatever it takes to keep the other person safe. And, if you recall, Michael was here for you as well when you suddenly found yourself in peril from your own federal employer."

"Yes, he was here, but then he disappeared afterwards and hasn't bothered to keep in touch over the last five years."

"He hasn't 'disappeared,' as you put it," Sam argued. "He went back to his family in San Francisco, and he certainly isn't in hiding. You could probably reach out to him if you wanted to make a connection. Just call his architectural firm and leave a message."

David considered this. "Well, that may seem a bit strange after all this time, and I couldn't be certain that he would be forthcoming about any questions that I asked. If I've learned anything over the years, Michael's a master of distraction and misdirection. He would be more open and honest with you."

"You're assuming quite a lot, David. I live my life here, and Michael lives his on the west coast. It's not as if we're 'besties' who constantly Facetime or text each other," Sam snorted. "Maybe it would be more expedient if you just told me what this 'problem' is."

So, David did. He explained about Senator Abrams' sudden appearance in David's home, and his insistence that Michael was up to his neck in something nefarious.

"He's hell-bent on finding him, Sam, and it's only a matter of time before he does because he's not above using any means, legal or otherwise. I'm certainly out of the loop on this one because I can't imagine what Michael has put into play to get that slimy creep's attention after all these years. What's the connection between those two?"

Of course, Sam Spade knew exactly what the connection was between Jarod Abrams and Michael, but he wasn't about to share that buried secret with David. Actually, only five people ever knew the true details, and two of those people were long dead and buried.

Many years ago, when old Philip Symington had taken a fifteen-year-old street kid into his home, he had Sam do an in-depth background check to find out the boy's story. It was Sam who had unearthed the sad facts of Michael's origin. His teenage mother had been impregnated by a young Jarod Abrams and then abandoned as the spoiled, selfish stud went on his merry way. The girl would later succumb to the lure of drugs a few years after giving birth. Michael only found out about his paternal father after Philip's death, and, eventually, he made Abrams aware of his existence.

So, unless Michael had decided to take someone else into his confidence, that left only three people who were currently in possession of the knowledge: Michael, Abrams, and Sam, himself. Sam knew there had to be more to this story and he was determined to unravel the mystery.

Chapter Eight

Sam's quick answer to David Parrish's question about the bond between himself and Michael was right on the money. They *always* had each other's backs. But it was also true that any communication between them was sporadic and sparse because they were both busy with their own lives. Of course, Sam was usually made aware of Michael's milestones. Several years ago, the young architect had called Sam with awe in his voice.

"It's unbelievable, Sam, really, really unbelievable—almost like a surreal out-of-body experience! Amy just presented me with the greatest gift that a wife could ever give her husband. Maybe I should have said 'gifts,' old buddy, because there are actually two of them. Amy and I have just enlarged our family by adding twin boys to the mix."

Sam couldn't have been happier for his friend who was a loving and devoted husband and father. Now Michael's little brood of nestlings was an amalgamation of Philip, Ella, and rambunctious Jeremy and Daniel. They all lived in a sort of controlled chaos in a rambling old San Francisco mansion on Steiner Street. Amy, Michael's wife, somehow managed to keep them all on track with the aid of a longtime and much-loved housekeeper named Amelia, and the children were also afforded a wealth of attention from doting grandparents and an attentive uncle.

Sam knew that Michael was truly happy at home as well as being fulfilled in his career choice. Many years ago, he had been made a full partner in his father-in-law's construction business, and his architectural creations vaulted that venture into a hugely profitable success. A young lost boy had grown up into a man who had somehow managed to grab the brass ring. Why would he ever want to revisit a painful past and stir up that hornet's nest? Sam supposed there was only one way to find out.

Amy Devereaux answered Sam's call, but there seemed to be some kind of loud shrieking in the background. He could hardly hear her over the noise, so she courteously excused herself for a second and placed her hand over the phone, but it wasn't enough to drown out her stern warning.

"You will *not* be kicking that ball in this house! Do you understand me, fellas? I will *not* repeat myself!"

"Sorry about that, Sam," she quickly apologized when she resumed their interrupted conversation. "The twins seem to think they're the ultimate jocks, so if there is anything that can be pitched, dribbled, or kicked, they're your men."

Sam couldn't help laughing. "It sounds as if you have your hands full, pretty lady, so hats off to you and your stamina. I certainly don't want to keep you from all the fun that you seem to be having, so I'd like to talk to your husband if he's available."

"Unfortunately, the ringmaster of this circus isn't here right now, Sam. He's been in Sydney, Australia all week for some kind of architectural conference. He's due back in a couple of days. Perhaps you can speak to him then unless it's some kind of emergency. I can give you the name of the hotel where he is staying if that's the case."

"No, no," Sam reassured her. "There's no emergency. I just need to talk to him about something. Would it be too much of an imposition if I foisted myself on you as a houseguest for perhaps a day or so when he gets home?"

"You know that you're always welcome, Sam, although you may want to bring along some Valium for survival purposes around this bunch," Amy laughed.

"Oh, I'm a tough old bird, and I've managed to live through much worse fates," Sam answered. "I'll see you and Michael sometime next week, Amy, and I'll be sure to be fortified with lots of Jack Daniels."

~~~~~~~~~

Even though Sam was forced to sit on his hands for the rest of the week, Jarod Abrams was not as idle. The day after the disgruntled man had left David Parrish's apartment, he had paid a visit to the Symington & Son import/export business in downtown Baltimore. Vincent Duffinetti, the owner, didn't seem pleased to see him because Abrams suspected that the Italian with Mafia ties had a lot to hide.

Abrams knew that Duffinetti had been Philip Symington's manager for decades in a business that was probably a front for smuggling stolen items that would later be sold on the black market. When old man Symington died, the business had been left to Michael Wyatt, but that could have been a carefully contrived red herring. Maybe Wyatt was the titular head, but the Mob most likely still controlled the flow of cash. That theory seemed the most plausible because when Michael inexplicably went AWOL from the scene, Vincent Duffinetti suddenly had the title to the whole shebang in his hands.

Abrams went straight for the jugular when he descended on Duffinetti.

"Where's Michael Wyatt? You had better be forthcoming, Duffinetti, because if you fuck with me, I promise to make your life and your paisans' lives a living hell. I'll sic the Feds on you again, and this time they'll find something that will stick!"

"You know, Senator, you remind me of the little mouse that roared," Duff snickered. "Pardon me if I don't take you too seriously and start shaking in my boots, but you're just a blowhard. If you want to bully somebody, go find some little old ladies who may actually be afraid of you."

"You'd better tell me where that slick son of a bitch is right now!" Abrams insisted.

"Is Michael missing?" Duff answered innocently. "Well, damn, maybe that's a mystery that you and your federal cronies will never figure out—sorta like the whereabouts of Jimmy Hoffa."

After he had expediently shut Abrams down and the angry Congressman had left, Duff placed a call to Sam.

"What's going on, Sam? Senator Jarod Abrams is suddenly gunning for Michael again, and he's out for bear. Why now after all these years?"

"I don't know, Duff, but I plan to find out," Sam promised.

"You'll let me know if I can help in any way," Duff replied earnestly. "I'm really fond of Michael and wouldn't want to see him become a victim of some evil megalomaniac with a vindictive agenda."

~~~~~~~~~~

Every damn person connected to Michael Wyatt seemed to be stonewalling, so Abrams had to rethink his search strategy. Of course, everybody who was anybody in Washington DC had connections. It was the way that business was conducted in the sometimes fiendishly devious realm of government. Money and power were the fluid currency that enticed flexible individuals to circumvent the laws of the land. Abrams then set about contacting an illegal hacker whom he knew would be discreet for the right price. He actually had the man on retainer to dig up dirt on fellow congressmen, lobbyists, and constituents that the Senator could use as leverage from time to time. It always assured him of continual re-election to his congressional seat. Now the hacker had a new assignment, and that was to search every national database for a Michael Wyatt sighting.

After a week of deep data-mining, the only thing that was unearthed was a complete dead end. The hacker had used Michael Wyatt's car registration from years ago to trace the vehicle that the missing man once owned. The old vintage Mercedes had been found abandoned in the huge Mall of America parking lot in Minnesota. Eventually, it was towed to a junkyard when no one came forth to claim it.

Abrams thought about this development. Minnesota wasn't far from the Canadian border. Now the desperate man was willing to grasp at any straw, no matter how flimsy. So, he told his hacker to continue his search internationally. That would probably prove to be a fruitless endeavor as well because the Senator began to suspect that Michael Wyatt was no longer Michael Wyatt. Now he was probably living as someone else.

Chapter Nine

The man who was now Michael Devereaux was glad to be coming home to his wife and family. Sydney was a fantastic and vibrant city with modern architecture that was sleek and visually appealing. However, the very heart of a husband and father resided in another dynamic city. He started to relax as soon as the Golden Gate Bridge came into view through the plane's small, rectangular window.

Homecomings were always sweet with his little clan of children clamoring to tell their father all that had happened in their youthful worlds during the time he was away. His wife was patient throughout their rambling discourses revolving around school activities, friends, and sports. Amy would later claim the precious night hours of Michael's attention. It was after some very sensuous endeavors that left both husband and wife sated and languid that she thought to inform him of Sam Spade's upcoming visit.

"Did he say why he suddenly decided to come?" Michael asked.

"No, he didn't. He just said that he wanted to talk to you about something. Since he's never been to our home before, maybe coming out here to California was simply something on his bucket list," Amy said thoughtfully.

"Maybe," Michael replied, but he wasn't truly convinced. He knew that Sam, an experienced and careful private investigator, was not one to indulge in anything that even hinted of spontaneity, so there had to be some reason that he wanted to see Michael in person. The man who now went by the name of

Michael Devereaux wondered if he should be worried. The next week, he would get his answer.

Sam had shown up at the door of the old "Painted Lady" mansion not long after his cross-country flight had touched down in San Francisco. He discovered that a lively welcoming committee was awaiting his arrival. Amy rushed to give the tall man a hug and plant an exuberant kiss on his cheek. She then hastily stepped back to allow Michael to add his own back-thumping embrace.

Sam peered over Michael's shoulder and found a somewhat younger audience staring up at him in fascination. Of course, there was Philip, now a tall and handsome 14-year-old with an engaging smile. The adolescent boy had fond memories of Sam from years ago, and now shyly stepped over to shake an old friend's hand.

Ella, his younger sister by five years, was next. The pretty little girl gave Sam a speculative and tentative once-over, and merely murmured a faint hello. Apparently, she had chosen to reserve her judgment of this stranger who was standing in front of her. The twins, four-year-olds Jeremy and Daniel, were like two identical peas in a pod with mischievous grins on their faces. They took turns introducing the new visitor to Francine the Golden Retriever and Dolores the white Angora cat. The whirlwind tour ended in their shared room where Hamilton and Hamish, the hamsters, were busy rustling the cedar shavings in their cages.

"We're a real menagerie, aren't we?" Amy said with a laugh as she and a smiling Michael looked on from the doorway. "Sorry if they overwhelmed you, Sam, but you're a new audience for them and they're never shy."

"Oh, it takes a lot to overwhelm an old war horse like me, so it's all good," Sam replied.

Later, as Sam sat down to dinner with the little group that now included Amelia, the housekeeper, he scanned the row of young faces around the table and marveled at how much they all looked like their father with his thick dark hair, chiseled cheekbones, and those arresting aquamarine eyes. They were a handsome lot, and Michael could never deny that they were his progeny. When the time was right, Sam was determined to discuss the specific genes on the family tree that had produced a young Michael many years ago.

~~~~~~~~~~

The next day found Michael and Sam seated on a bench at the Botanical Gardens in Golden Gate Park.

"Okay, Sam," Michael began, "lay it on me. I know you well enough that I'm not buying that you just suddenly decided to drop in for a social visit. What's the problem?"

Sam looked serious as he answered with a just name, "Jarod Abrams."

Michael looked perplexed. "Wow! That's a blast from a past that I thought I had left far behind in Baltimore. Exactly how is he a problem now?"

"Well, he's making himself a real pain in the ass these days because, for some reason, he really wants to find you again. The Senator is making the rounds in Baltimore. He's gone to Manus Kirschner, David Parrish, and even Duff. Actually, he wound up threatening Duff, and I think he means business. He hasn't gotten my scent yet, and I don't see how he could. Philip Symington and I had an off-the-books kind of deal in place. It was all done with cash, and I left no trace of myself behind."

"Why is the man suddenly looking for me now?" Michael wondered. "I remember that he always had an agenda back in the day, and I can't imagine that has changed. The question is, what does he think he'll be gaining by finding me again?"

"So, you didn't do anything to wind him up?" Sam asked.

"No!" Michael assured Sam. "That's the last thing that I'd ever want to do."

"Well, he told David Parrish that you were up to your old tricks, and he intended to put a stop to your plans. What do you think he was referring to as 'your plans'?"

"Actually, long ago in the distant past, I did provide him with concrete DNA evidence to convince him that I was his biological son. You're a smart man, Sam, so you probably guessed at the time that it was a type of social blackmail to persuade him to represent me against all the federal charges that were raining down on my head. Is he claiming that I'm blackmailing him now?"

"He hasn't been forthcoming enough to specify why you have become his 'flavor of the month,' but it could very well be something along those lines. Or maybe the son of a bitch desperately needs a kidney from a relative. Who else knows that he is your father besides me?"

"Nobody," Michael swore adamantly. "I certainly wouldn't want to open that can of worms."

"You never told Amy?" Sam asked.

"I did tell Amy the very broad strokes about my life back in Baltimore before we were married, but I never provided actual names for all the characters in that terrible melodrama. I only told her about Philip Symington, David Parrish, and, you, of course. But, Amy would never share that information, not even with her family."

"Well, at least you're now forewarned about what may be coming down the pike," Sam mused. "Maybe you should try to keep a low profile for the time being and not get your face on another 'Architectural Digest' magazine cover in the near future. I'll keep you posted from my end."

"Thanks, Sam. I owe you," Michael answered.

"Didn't think that we were keeping score, Buddy," Sam said fondly as he punched Michael lightly on the shoulder.

~~~~~~~~~~

One month later, it seemed as if Jarod Abrams was making good on his threats. Sam reported that Manus Kirshner had been forced to turn over the financial records of "The Haven" to a forensic accountant who was diligently trying to ferret out the source of the revenue that was initially used to build it. Likewise, the Feds had descended on "Symington & Son" and were tearing their invoice files apart as well. To add insult to injury, the New York City police were interviewing a former violinist associated with the Baltimore Symphony Orchestra who claimed that David Parrish's wife, Bunny, had arranged for him to be assaulted and maimed after he had broken up with her.

"That vile snake needs to crawl back into the hole that he slithered out of," Sam complained. "He's doing everything in his power to flush you out. What bug could he have up his friggin' ass after all these years? He has as much on the line as you do if it ever gets out that he is your father."

"Maybe it's about time that I find out what's lit a fire under him," Michael replied. "I can't just sit back and let him try to destroy the people that I care about so that I can stay under the radar. He's my problem, not theirs."

"Be extremely careful, Michael. Abrams is beyond devious, and he's always thinking of ways to screw people. This may be some kind of slick trap that he's luring you into for his own personal gain. Most likely, it's probably twisted and perverse on every level."

"I'm definitely not going to argue that point, Sam, because you're theory is probably right on the money. Therefore, I think that I'm just going to suddenly show up on the Senator's doorstep and pay him a little unannounced visit," Michael explained. "When I miraculously appear, I can only hope that he won't have an opportunity to put any panic measures into play. After I get the lay of the land regarding his new sudden interest in me, I'll try to initiate some contingencies to thwart his agenda. Actually, this is really a fly-by-the-seat-of-my-pants strategy, but I can't think of anything else to do at the moment."

Sam grunted as he added to the discussion. "I just happen to know that the Senator keeps a small, luxury apartment right in the heart of DC. He spends most of his time there— really much more than he spends at his home in Baltimore. Some people, who are not above gossiping, call it his 'love nest' 'cause, apparently, he seems to really like the ladies, and the younger the better."

"Yeah, he had a similar reputation when he was a lawyer in Baltimore," Michael agreed. "Of course, that certainly could have been idle gossip, as well," he added cynically.

"Maybe I should shadow you when you have your little reunion with your sperm donor, Michael. Just tell me a date and a time and I'm there," Sam offered.

"I'll be fine, Buddy. I'll hear what's on his conniving little mind and then I'll stop back in Baltimore to give you a heads up before I fly home," Michael promised.

"Are you sure?" Sam asked earnestly.

"Yeah, I'm sure. What could possibly happen?"

Chapter Ten

Before Michael left to fly across the country on his fact-finding mission, he had a heart-to-heart talk with his wife. This time he provided a lot more detail about his origins.

"My mother, Jessica Anderson, was just sixteen-years-old when Abrams impregnated her," he explained to Amy. "To put that into perspective, that's only two years older than Philip is now. She was young and naïve and probably very afraid when she suddenly found herself alone without a safety net. Everyone, including her parents and lover boy, had abandoned her. I'm not condoning her use of drugs, but maybe I understand why she went down that road and eventually abandoned me."

"Michael, you're being a lot more forgiving than I would be in your situation," Amy declared vehemently. "I'm a mother, and I would *never* abandon my child for any reason on this earth. Each of my children are a part of me that I carried under my heart for nine months. I gave them life. It's just not a normal maternal instinct to throw that life away."

Michael answered her with a fond expression on his face. This was the woman whom he loved with all of his heart and soul. She was an unwavering and supportive spouse as well as a devoted mother who would protect her offspring as ferociously as a mother bear protects her cubs.

"Our past is our past, Sweetheart. It's over and done and nobody can change what happened to them during that time. To stay sane, you have to eventually come to terms with it, and then let it go and move on so that it doesn't consume you. You also can't use it as a cop out or an excuse for the person that you later become. Your actions are personal choices that you make rather than a preordained destiny because of your genes. So, I jettisoned all that ugly baggage a long time ago—or at least I thought that I had."

"So, you never wanted to find out who your biological father was?" his wife asked.

"Not when I was a kid. I had a chip on my shoulder, and decided that if the jerk hadn't wanted me, then I certainly didn't want anything to do with whomever he was. However, after Philip Symington passed away, he left that genealogical information for me, and I was finally mature enough to handle it."

"Did Jarod Abrams know that he had a son—you? If he didn't, then how did he find out that you even existed?" Amy asked the next logical question.

"Well, that's on me," Michael admitted. "I wasn't exactly leading an exemplary life when I was a young adult back in Baltimore. The Feds eventually investigated my business and filed a slew of charges against me. During that period, Jarod Abrams had cleverly managed to make a name for himself as a very successful attorney. It was then that I made him aware that I was his biological son. He grudgingly represented me in court and I was found 'not guilty' of everything.

I certainly didn't delude myself into thinking that he had done that out of any paternal concern. I don't think that he ever told anyone of our connection, and he made it crystal clear that he wanted me to disappear from his life after the trial was over. So, it wasn't long after that ordeal when I gladly accommodated his wish by doing exactly that."

"And now he's suddenly trying to find you," Amy stated the obvious.

"And going about it in a threatening way," Michael added. "I really have to get to the bottom of this, Amy, to see what his motivation is. To tell you the truth, I can't imagine that it's anything good."

"No, it probably isn't," she agreed. "I'll bet Sam told you about this, didn't he, when he came for that impromptu visit a month ago. Please tell me that he'll watch your back when you have your reunion with your father, Michael, because it sounds dangerous. Maybe this Senator Abrams somehow now perceives you as a threat, and knows that he will lose a lot of credibility if the facts were ever divulged. Maybe that's why he's reacting in kind."

"I've got this, Darlin', so please stop worrying," Michael said earnestly. "There's nothing that this man can do to me that he didn't already do after I was conceived. I certainly don't wish him any harm, but, on the other hand, I can't, in good faith, wish him well either. I just want him to stop badgering people who are important to me. That's going to take an in-your-face encounter."

And that's just what happened a few nights later.

Chapter Eleven

It was the early days of January and frigidly cold and bleak in Washington DC. Michael sat in his rented sedan and buttoned up his black overcoat as he waited at the curb outside of Jarod Abrams' posh apartment building near Dupont Circle. Winter had brought an early darkness, and it now felt like the middle of the night even though it was barely 8 pm. Michael had chosen the evening for his rendezvous with the man who was his father. He wanted to be certain that the Congressman was at home for the night and not hobnobbing with his Senate cronies in some upscale restaurant. He noted that there were lights visible in the apartment that faced the street on the eighth level. Taking a deep breath, he knew it was now or never that he had to confront the problem head on.

There was no doorman protecting the gates of the entitled, so Michael took the single elevator to the correct floor. There was another older man in the lobby who accompanied him in the car as it slowly ascended, and they each afforded the other a courteous nod before turning to face forward again. The fellow passenger remained inside as Michael stepped out onto the eighth floor. A determined man then put his finger on the buzzer outside of his father's apartment and purposely bowed his head so that Abrams couldn't ascertain who was standing in the hall. When the unsuspecting man opened his door to find his firstborn son on the threshold, he uttered an angry curse.

"You son of a bitch!"

"Perhaps a more accurate aspersion would have been, 'You bastard,'" Michael quickly answered the slur as he pushed his way into the apartment and looked around curiously.

"Well, it seems like you've done well for yourself, 'Dad,'" he snarked as he boldly strode around the space perusing the expensive furniture and paintings on the wall while an irate and scowling man trailed in his wake. Michael finally stopped his casual meandering at a granite island in the kitchen where he picked up an open bottle of 25-year-old single malt Scotch.

"Of course, nothing but the best for the illustrious Senator Jarod Abrams," he mocked. "You're a man who wants what he wants because he thinks that's his due, and you'll stop at nothing until you get it. You don't allow anybody to get in your way. If they do, you just steamroll right over them and leave them in the dust like a bit of collateral damage. Jessica Anderson, my mother, was collateral damage to you, and now, apparently, I have suddenly become an impediment to some grand plan that he have for yourself. I think that you owe me an explanation."

"Don't act as if you don't know what you are doing to me," Abrams barked. "You're trying to ruin me by bleeding me dry. You're the same deceitful and conniving cur that you were years ago. What made you finally have the guts to do your dirty work in person?"

Michael cocked his head curiously.

"Unfortunately, you have me at a disadvantage, because I have absolutely no idea what you're raving about. Please, by all means, enlighten me."

Instead of an immediate answer, the older man snatched some papers off the adjacent kitchen counter and slammed them down in front of Michael.

"Don't act as if this is all a shocking surprise to you, Wyatt, since you're obviously behind this disgusting travesty!"

Michael's eyes narrowed as he quickly scanned copies of several emails sent to Jason and Justin Abrams at their college Internet addresses. The barrage of terse messages documented a progressively mounting extortion scheme, and the latest demand had the hush money's price tag up to twenty-five thousand dollars. They were all signed "Michael."

Abrams' unacknowledged son actually smiled as he turned to answer his ranting father.

"Well, I do believe that the cunning and duplicitous Senator Abrams has met his match for deviousness. You, Senator, have succumbed to a pretty nifty con job. My hat is off to the intrepid soul who dared to take you on, but, unfortunately, that idiotically brash person isn't me. I have told no one about our relationship because it actually makes me feel ashamed to own it. So, if there is a leak—and obviously there is—then it has to have come from your end, old man. Maybe you need to get your own house in order because someone is playing you. How does it feel to be on the receiving end for once?"

"You're a fucking liar, Wyatt, just like you always were. You want to ruin me," Abrams spat.

Michael just shook his head cynically.

"If I truly wanted to ruin you, I could have done that years ago while you were a state's attorney, or in private practice, or even when you clawed your way up the political ladder to becoming a senator. I could have sold my sad and poignant little story to the scandal sheets and you wouldn't have looked so squeaky clean then. I even had the DNA evidence to prove my claim. However, I certainly didn't need blackmail money then, nor do I need it now. In fact, the only thing that I need from you, Senator, is an end to this ridiculously paranoid crusade against innocent people."

Abrams suddenly was right in Michael's face.

"You can deny all that you want, but I know that you're as twisted and perverted as that old homo back in Baltimore who took you in. Did Symington turn you into his own personal little faggot that he nailed every chance he got?"

Without thinking, Michael brought up his clenched fist and connected with Abrams' cheekbone, sending the unfortunate man to the floor with a crash.

Michael stood over him menacingly and softly added his own threatening words.

"You had better rethink what you have put into motion, Senator, because you'll find that I can give as good as I get. Don't force me to descend to your level!"

After their volatile interaction had reached its climax, an enraged Michael turned on his heel and slammed the door behind him as he quickly exited the apartment. Once back in his rented car, an angry man pummeled his already bruised fist against the steering wheel and fought hard to get himself under control. When he had sufficiently calmed down, he made an illegal U-turn on the street and sped towards the interstate highway that would take him out of this city and far away from the lingering stench of his biological father.

He hadn't gone but a few blocks before he saw flashing lights in his rearview mirror. Sighing deeply, he immediately pulled over. After what seemed like an eternity, a swaggering and scowling metro cop sauntered over and demanded to see his registration and driver's license. The officer carefully examined the documents with close scrutiny, wrote Michael a vehicular violation for the illegal turn as well as exceeding the district's speed ordinance, and ominously warned him to obey all traffic signs and speed limits during the rest of his stay in the nation's capital. Michael did just that as he made his way towards Baltimore and his meeting with Sam.

Chapter Twelve

"So, what's his game?" Sam wanted to know when Michael made it back to the private detective's apartment that night in Baltimore. After Sam's previous home had gone up in flames a few years ago, the displaced man had taken up residence in the Symington Place complex near the harbor.

"Somebody is blackmailing him because somehow they have come into the knowledge that I'm his real illegitimate son that he abandoned," Michael explained. "The demands were delivered via his college-age sons, and, apparently, he has already paid some hush money to keep it quiet. However, as everyone knows, blackmailers are greedy, and they're never done with you. They'll continue to return to that well time and time again. The emails that the boys received were signed 'Michael,' so it seems as if somebody really does know the whole story, and Abrams assumed that it was me doing the extorting."

"Ah, so the evil past sins of the father have come home to plague his supposedly sanctimonious life. How appropriate!" Sam said.

"Yeah, well it couldn't have happened to a more deserving guy," Michael agreed. "I tried to tell him that the demands definitely hadn't come from me, but he wasn't buying it, so, unfortunately, he's still a threat."

Sam eyed the raw abrasion and the surrounding bruise on Michael's right hand.

"I take it that you tried very strenuously to convince him otherwise."

Michael had the grace to look a bit sheepish. "Maybe I did try to drive home my point a little vigorously."

"Took a page out of David Parrish's book, did you?" Sam teased.

"Maybe," Michael agreed. "Nevertheless, right now, while I'm in town, I need to touch base with him and Duff and Manus to let them know just what the nasty Senator is trying to do. I suppose that I owe them a plausible explanation of the why. I don't need to clarify all the actual facts surrounding the witch-hunt. I'll just say that it's all a misconception on the Senator's end about my past deeds and leave it at that."

~~~~~~~~~~

Early the next day, Michael's first stop was the law firm of Kirshner and Faraday, and since it was the afternoon of Mrs. Kirshner's book club meeting, he found the old attorney nodding off behind his desk at the office while the stock market ticker-tape scrolled across the screen of a nearby television. He surged awake when the secretary announced Michael's presence.

"My God, I can't believe that it's you," the old man growled as he embraced Michael fondly. "It's been years and you look as sophisticated and debonair as you did eons ago when you suddenly left town. I wondered at first where you had gone, but then, down the road, I figured it out. You see, the office tries to keep upscale reading material in the waiting room for our discriminating clients. 'Architectural Digest' is one such publication, so imagine my surprise when I saw your very handsome face on the front cover. Tell me, how do you like San Francisco, my boy?"

"Hello, Manus," Michael finally managed to get out. "It's really good to see you, too, and I don't mind saying that San

Francisco is a fabulous city where I've managed to put down roots after I left Baltimore behind. Now I'm back for just a brief visit, although I only wish that it was under better circumstances."

"Surely you're not referring to that brouhaha that Jarod Abrams is trying to get off the ground. That idiot is a tempest in a teapot and actually a laughable clown," Manus assured Michael with a dismissive wave of his hand.

"Nevertheless, he is making some trouble for 'The Haven,'" Michael said worriedly.

"I can assure you, young man, that the books for that institution are impeccable. As for the funds that made it possible all those years ago, well, I can finagle with the best of them, and I have taken care of that minor problem quite handily. I simply added a codicil to Philip Symington's will, backdated it, and then had it duly notarized and witnessed after I very cleverly added my old friend's very passable signature. That document put a substantial portion of Philip's estate into a trust with the stipulation that it would be used to construct a refuge for the poor abused children of Baltimore. It will stand up to the most intense scrutiny, so please stop worrying. Now, make an old man happy and tell me what's gotten old Jarod into such a tizzy to find you after all these years."

"Apparently, somebody has some dirt on him and has been blackmailing him with that sordid knowledge. He thinks that it's me," Michael explained succinctly.

Manus actually cackled. "I have lived my whole life here in Baltimore, Michael, and if anyone knows about old skeletons in dark closets, it's yours truly. Abrams has so many skeletons by now that he probably has to rent a storage locker to house them all. Did you perhaps stumble onto one of them while he

47

was representing you at trial way back in the day, and now you're enjoying a little payback while you make him sweat?"

"That may have been very tempting," Michael admitted, "but, no, I'm not the source of his grief. I tried to tell him that, but I don't think he believed me."

"More's the pity," the old attorney answered. "However, he deserves to get a dose of his own medicine because he's used delicate information in the past to boost himself to the top of the political heap. He's in his element, and probably enjoys keeping company with like-minded individuals who are as corrupt as he is. The government is full of those kinds of two-faced scum. I hope that the slippery Senator has to part ways with a ton of his money before this thing runs its course."

~~~~~~~~~~

Michael's next visit an hour later was to Vincent Duffinetti's condo down near Baltimore's Inner Harbor. Just like Manus, the old Italian assured Michael that there was no danger to himself or to Symington & Son.

"This isn't our first rodeo, Michael, and we know how to play the game because we have been doing it since Philip Symington was at the helm. We'll just let the Feds keep spinning their wheels while we laugh our asses off at all their feeble-mindedness. Now, if you need us to shut the little twerp down, we can certainly help you out with that."

Michael knew exactly how the Mob would accomplish the deed, and it wasn't a pretty picture.

"Thanks for the generous offer, Duff, but I need to handle this myself. I've already had a heart-to-heart talk with him, so maybe I've convinced him to cease and desist."

Duff smiled as he changed the subject. "So, how's your family?"

Suddenly, Michael found himself invited to dinner with Duff and his wife, Carla, and he added yet another day to his stay in Baltimore.

Chapter Thirteen

On Wednesday, Michael had his return flight home to San Francisco booked for later in the evening, so he used the afternoon to make one last stop. It wasn't long before he found himself knocking on yet another door and waiting patiently in the hall. When the occupant finally responded and stood in front of him, Michael smiled.

"Hello, David," he said softly.

"Hello, Michael," David Parrish answered with a frown and crossed arms.

"Wow, you really don't seem very happy to see me again," Michael hazarded a guess.

David raised his eyebrow and answered in a cynical tone.

"Every time that you suddenly show up on my doorstep, Buster, I usually find myself getting dragged into one of your convoluted donnybrooks. That last time I almost got killed for my efforts, so tell me I'm wrong to be a bit hesitant to break out the party hats and balloons at your arrival today."

"Now that attitude is truly hurtful, David" Michael replied. "We used to work well together back in the day. As for the last caper, if you let yourself remember accurately, you'll recall that I was the one who actually saved your life that night. And, if it wasn't for me, you would have never met your lovely wife."

"Well, there is that," David admitted as he ushered Michael into the living room.

"Hey, you still have the cat," Michael marveled as he spied the orange tabby splayed atop a stack of papers next to an open laptop.

"Yep—I still have my cat. Now, please tell me why you're here because I know it means trouble."

Michael ignored the direct query and rambled on.

"By the way, congrats on your many literary achievements, David. I've read every one of your novels and I'm impressed. Correct me if I'm wrong, but some of the plots remind me of a past harrowing experience with the evil political industrial complex. But then, it's like they say—a good author writes about what he knows."

"Michael, you're deflecting," David harrumphed. "Just tell me the real reason for this impromptu visit."

Michael sighed—so much for catching up with idle chit chat.

"It's regarding your wife," he began. "I heard through my sources that Senator Jarod Abrams is encouraging some jerk in New York to resurrect old accusations about a terrible mishap that befell him when he once played here in the Baltimore Symphony."

David's eyes suddenly narrowed. "So, that's where that whole ridiculous thing originated. I should have had my own suspicions when he tried to pump me for your whereabouts. Why was the wily Senator Abrams even interested in you, and why was he willing to go to such lengths to find you? What mess have you gotten yourself into this time?"

"Well, that's a story for another day, and it's really very boring," Michael answered. "Where's Bunny, by the way? I should be apologizing to her."

Even though David was distracted, he smiled fondly at the mention of his wife.

"She's touring Austria with the Symphony and is not due back for several weeks. I haven't even made her aware of all this nonsense regarding her old flame. Bunny had nothing to do with causing him any injuries, so I don't want her to be upset over something that is going nowhere. The statute of limitations is three years for assault, and we're way past that now. The guy's only recourse will be a civil suit, and he'd be hard pressed to prove anything. In fact, Bunny could counter-sue for all the broken bones and concussions that she suffered at his hands way back then. That's a hard fact that's all documented by the hospitals that treated her time and time again."

Michael seemed relieved and started for the door.

"Please tell Bunny that I'm sorry that I missed her," he said over his shoulder. "And, just so you know, it was good to see you again, David."

The older man wasn't about to let his visitor leave just yet. He quickly grabbed onto Michael's forearm as he reached for the doorknob.

"Michael, I think you've gotten yourself into some very big trouble concerning Senator Abrams," he stated forcefully.

"No, I haven't," Michael said in denial. "I actually went to see the Congressman in Washington before I stopped here. I made it very clear to him that he was operating under some misconceptions. I believe that he got the message. I took care of the problem, and I don't think the Senator will be bothering anyone anymore."

David's heart actually skipped a beat at Michael's turn of phrase, and alarm bells started clanging in his head. He knew that he had to ask the question even though he was suddenly terrified of the answer that he might hear.

"Do I want to know how you convinced him to back off?" he asked apprehensively.

"Probably not," Michael admitted.

David stared into his visitor's suddenly guileless blue eyes for a few silent heartbeats before he dropped his bombshell.

"Michael, there was a breaking news bulletin on the air a few minutes ago, and it concerned Jarod Abrams. Somebody murdered him in his apartment on Monday evening! Now, tell me the truth. Did you kill him, Michael?" he asked softly.

If it wasn't so tragic, it might have been comical to watch Michael's cocky expression turn to one of appalled shock that looked truly genuine. David intently studied the suddenly pale man before him. He needed to have Michael actually look him in the eye when he answered David's direct question.

"Did you kill him?" David repeated.

"No, no," the younger man finally whispered, "we argued, but he was alive when I left. I swear, David, he was okay when I left him."

Sometimes, you just had to go with your gut, and since David's hadn't yet begun spewing out rivers of acid to convince him otherwise, he decided to believe the seemingly dumbfounded man in front of him. Maybe he was a fool, and perhaps he always had been when it came to Michael. He certainly was aware of the hair trigger temper, the reckless impetuous acts, and the ensuing pathos that, even as a young man, he had left in his wake. However, this time there was no waffling. Michael had emphatically denied being the Senator's assassin. During their past relationship, the younger man had been known to be cagey and to irritatingly sidestep an admission by withholding pertinent information. However, when asked directly, he had never yet lied to David.

The older man finally nodded his head and decided to step off a cliff.

"Okay, I believe you, Michael. So, unless you're in a hurry to get out of town because the cops are on your tail, why don't we sit for a while so that you can be more specific about what actually happened on Monday night. C'mon, Picasso, paint me a picture!"

Chapter Fourteen

Michael had a lot to think about as his flight home left the Baltimore runway behind. He admitted to himself that, at first, it really had been good to see David again. Although their relationship had always had its ups and downs, when they found themselves in the trenches, they looked out for one another. The bond had been forged way back when Michael was just a kid looking for an idol, and it had remained intact time and again when he was a young adult. Michael knew that David tended to bend the rules a bit for him, but the sometimes impulsively headstrong man was also aware there were limits to his friend's flexibility. If Michael went too far afield, David would jerk him back from the precipice before he reached the point of no return. He could only hope that David had believed him today.

Then Michael's thoughts turned to home and his wife and children. He wondered if, or perhaps when, a connection would be made linking two different Michaels. Everything that he valued as Michael Devereaux was there awaiting him in San Francisco. If his parentage was suddenly revealed back east, that was just a raw fact which meant nothing to him because it didn't define whom he had become. It had absolutely no value, and it didn't make him feel ashamed or diminished.

It was his biological father who should have felt disgraceful guilt for his irresponsibility and the lack of compassion that he had displayed a long time ago. Michael just could not fathom abandoning one of his own children or denying their existence because each one was a precious gift that enriched his life day after day.

To be honest, Michael had always felt like an orphan. Jarod Abrams had never really been his father, so he deserved every bit of angst that this unknown blackmailer had caused him. However, Michael wasn't sure if the man had deserved to die because of that information.

Finally, in an effort to dull his thoughts, Michael reclined his seat and put on headphones for the rest of the flight. It was much later that he was jolted awake from a light sleep as the announcement was made to fasten seat belts and return the trays to an upright and locked position. The jumbo jet touched down soon after, and then screeched along the runway as the pilot applied the brakes of the big bird. It was a smooth landing, and the plane sedately taxied to the proper docking station.

Michael only had a carry-on piece of luggage, so he skirted the downstairs carousels and exited the airport. He was about to text Amy to ask if she had arrived yet to pick him up when he quickly spotted her and her brother, Lawrence, waving and smiling, just across the cement median that ran along the drop-off and pick-up lanes. He was about to wave back when, suddenly, at least six San Francisco Police officers swarmed around him shouting his name with their guns at the ready. Two got behind him and yanked his arms behind his back before applying tight manacles. Another was telling him quite forcefully that he, Michael Devereaux, was under arrest for the murder of Senator Jarod Abrams in Washington DC!

Michael wasn't even listening to his Miranda rights. He was frantically searching for Amy's face in a curious crowd that had suddenly assembled. When their eyes finally met, he saw that her's were wide with shocked fear, but there was also an unspoken question in them. He looked at her intently and moved his head slightly from side to side. It was an almost undetectable brief motion, and most likely, it was only his wife who was aware of their silent communication. Amy had her answer, but it did nothing to allay her fear. She seemed to be frozen in that moment in time.

It was Lawrence Buchanan, Michael's brother-in-law, and, serendipitously, also a criminal lawyer, who recovered his wits the fastest.

"I'm this man's attorney," he bellowed loudly as he pushed his way into the scrum. "Don't say another word, Michael."

Part Two – Three Days Earlier
Chapter Fifteen

The initial frantic call had come into the desk sergeant at Washington's Second District Police Station House at 11 am on an otherwise dull Tuesday. However, that was all about to change. Mrs. Sheila Abrams, Senator Jarod Abrams' wife, was calling from their home in Maryland, and, to put it mildly, she was exceedingly distraught. However, her frazzled state of mind certainly didn't prevent her from being demanding.

"I am extremely worried about my husband, the Senator, and I want someone to check on his welfare right now!"

The old desk sergeant sighed. Unfortunately, he was used to dealing with political figures and diplomats as well as their families who thought that they were some kind of royalty.

"Ma'am, are you saying that Senator Abrams is missing?" he asked calmly.

"What I am saying is that he didn't answer his phone at all last night, and he's also not responding to the texts that I've sent," she enunciated slowly as if talking to an imbecile.

The jaded officer imagined that if he had a shrew like this woman dogging his every move, maybe he might pretend deafness, too, so that he could ignore her. Of course, that wasn't exactly his response.

"Mrs. Abrams, perhaps your husband's phone has a dead battery, or maybe he has the volume turned off and he didn't hear your calls and messages. Did you try again this morning or call his Senate office?"

"Of course, I did!" she almost shrieked. "I was informed by his secretary that he actually missed a roll call vote in the Senate earlier today, and nobody knows where he is. I want someone to go to his apartment to reassure me that he is alright, and I want that done immediately."

"Of course, Mrs. Abrams. We'll look into that right away," the desk sergeant answered deferentially. "Now, if you'll be good enough to tell me his address, I'll send two officers to go and knock on his door."

"That's not good enough by any stretch of the imagination," she proclaimed haughtily. "I don't want just any beat cops knocking and ringing the Senator's buzzer. That might send the wrong message to any nosey neighbors who may be nasty enough to start ugly rumors.

No, uniformed officers won't do at all. I insist that you to send plain clothes detectives in suits to his apartment located off of Dupont Circle. It's not as if I'm asking them to travel to the moon and back. That area is well within your jurisdiction. If my husband still isn't responding, then I want them to get the master key from the management and have a look inside.

Senator Abrams is a middle-aged man, so it's possible that he could have suffered a heart attack or a stroke. He could have eaten some foreign spice or herb at an upscale fusion restaurant and suffered a fatal allergic reaction. Perhaps he is lying unconscious or dying on the floor. There are just too many horrible things to even contemplate."

"Of course, Mrs. Abrams, you're quite right," the sergeant commiserated without a hint of cynicism in his tone. "That must be very worrisome for you and I'll get some detectives on it right away."

After hanging up, the put-upon older man heaved another peevish sigh. He gazed around him and spied newly-arrived Detective Jesse Cormier sauntering across the room trying to balance two cups of coffee and a McDonald's carryout sack in his hands.

"Hey Jesse," he called to the good old boy transplant from Louisiana. "I do believe you're up next for an assignment. It seems as if I'm gonna have to send you and your partner on a fool's errand. Some senator's wife is complaining that her husband went AWOL and she wants us to check out his apartment."

"Seriously?" the creole detective whined in annoyance. "I seem to recall when I was living down South that this here place was said to be rife with real crime. How's this even compute?"

"Yeah, well regardless of our rather outstanding reputation regarding illegal acts here in the District, we gotta keep all the little local demigods happy so that they can continue to make the world go round and round," the sergeant snarked.

"Exactly who ran away to join the circus?" Cormier wanted to know.

"Senator Jarod Abrams over off of Dupont Circle."

Cormier made a face. "That dude has a reputation as a real hound dog, always sniffing around the ladies. I also heard he's an arrogant putz."

The desk sergeant grimaced. "Please tell me exactly how a redneck hillbilly like you even knows the Yiddish word for prick."

"Well, my good buddy, when you're married to a Jewish American princess, the swear words are the first ones that you do learn," the detective grinned mischievously.

Actually, Jesse Cormier was an easygoing, happily married man with two teenage children. He had an acerbic, quick wit and a determined attitude when he was on the job. He and his partner closed more of their cases than they left unsolved

59

because, although a mismatched set, they complimented each other in many ways.

Cormier's partner was swarthy and stoic Attiq Kabli, a third generation Arab-American whose familial roots went back several generations to Morocco. Sometime in the last century, a great-grandfather had emigrated through Ellis Island and embraced the dream of a better life, and he made it happen through hard work and perseverance. Modern day Attiq had his ancestor's drive, and it didn't hurt that he looked like a young, handsome Omar Sharif.

Jesse extended a paper coffee cup to Attiq and put the bag containing Egg McMuffins on the desks that separated them.

"I come bearing gifts, Partner, but also some bad news. You and I have been ordered to do a 'fun run' over to Dupont Circle. Believe it or not, one of our dedicated congressmen, Senator Jarod Abrams, is not being responsive to one of his loyal constituents. In this case, it's his wife that he's ducking, and I'm not sure if our job descriptions include marriage counseling."

"Justitia Omnibus," Attiq said solemnly, "is the motto emblazoned on our police badges. That's Latin for 'Justice For All.' Perhaps Mrs. Abrams would like her justice served up by two obedient Metro public servants. If we manage to surprise the wayward guy in the sack with some babe, wifey would have herself two unimpeachable witnesses at the divorce trial," he concluded with a straight face.

"There just may be a method to the lady's madness," Jesse agreed. "Let's have breakfast before we make the trek to 'Marriage Boot Camp.'"

Chapter Sixteen

Unfortunately, their current problem didn't have an easy fix. Repeated knocking and buzzing at Senator Abrams' door produced no sleepy Lothario. The two detectives then flashed their badges at the building's supervisor on the ground floor, and the man grudgingly obliged by accompanying them to the elevator where they slowly ascended to the eighth floor.

On the ride up, Attiq remarked, "I'm surprised an upscale building like this doesn't have a doorman."

The man looked back at the detective dolefully. "Our own federal government has to make budget cuts all the time or else the whole overblown system is in danger of shutting down. If they can't find a way to stop the bleeding for military funding and the handout programs, then they send a lot of people home on a brief, temporary furlough. We got financial troubles here, too, so the guys who own the building trim expenditures where they can. Our doorman didn't have the privilege of being temporarily furloughed. The poor dude got permanently canned. So, now we're left with one security camera outside the front door and one camera in this elevator, and that's as good as it gets."

Then the man's curiosity got the better of him.

"How come you need to get into the Senator's apartment? Has he done something sketchy and you guys want to poke around. Don't you need a search warrant for that?"

"Nah," Jesse assured him. "His wife called us from out of state and she's worried that he might be sick or something. We'll just take a quick peek to make sure he's not there, and we don't need to touch a thing. Listen, buddy, if this makes you nervous, you can call the lady to square it with her."

"Well, you are the police, so I guess it's alright. I just don't want the Senator to be mad at me if he finds out."

"Chill, man—it's all good," the detective reassured him.

Jesse and Attiq retraced their steps to the correct door and stood back as the manager used a master key to open it. When the two detectives sauntered inside calling the Senator's name, they eventually found that their mundane day had suddenly taken on a new dimension.

Jarod Abrams' body was lying face up on the kitchen floor. His skin was pasty white, most likely because he probably didn't have any blood left in his corpse. The average human body contains approximately five liters of blood, and that entire amount seemed to be pooled on the kitchen tiles around his head and shoulders. It was dark, almost black in color, and well on its way to congealing into a rather gelatinous mess. The detectives took a cautious look and saw the jagged gash in his neck.

"His carotid was probably severed, and the arterial spray would have been like a geyser," Attiq hazarded a guess. "By the consistency of the blood, it looks like he's been down for a while, maybe even since last night. It also looks as if he was about to pour himself a stiff one when he got whacked."

The detective had noted a glass tumbler on the kitchen island. A multitude of glass shards and an almost intact center portion of a pricey bottle of Scotch lay on the floor on the other side of the kitchen near the sink.

"Yeah, that seems about right to me," Jesse agreed. "So now we know why the Senator wasn't answering his phone. But it doesn't tell us anything yet about how he ended up like this. Since we didn't see any signs of forced entry, we'll have to assume that the dead man allowed his murderer into his apartment. Maybe the unsub had a gun and forced his way in, but that doesn't compute because if a home invader meant the guy harm, why not just shoot him using a silencer?"

"I hear ya, Partner," Attiq nodded his head in agreement. "It looks like maybe there could have been an altercation here in the kitchen between two people who knew each other, and there was a spat that got out of hand. If the pissed off assailant didn't bring a weapon, then he had to implement on the fly and use what was already here and handy."

The two detectives knew that speculating would get them nowhere at this point in time. They needed more information. So, the familiar drill was activated, and phone calls were made to various units. A police photographer took a multitude of pictures of the corpse in situ as well as meticulously photographing the entire crime scene and the adjacent rooms. Then the coroner did his thing by formally declaring the Senator "dead." He next used the most basic of his tools to determine liver temperature so that he could offer his best guess as to when the senator had ceased to exist.

"I can give you an unsubstantiated estimate that this man has been dead at least twelve to fourteen hours, but the autopsy should be more definitive. I can, however, tell you, without a doubt, that he exsanguinated from the jagged wound to his neck. There was one sharp swipe that connected with his carotid. The cut is jagged, and even though I couldn't say for sure until I get him on the table, I would venture a guess that it may have been accomplished with a big shard of glass from that broken bottle. Collect all the pieces and I'll try to find a match."

Jesse and Attiq knew that if murder cases weren't solved quickly within the initial first forty-eight hours, trails grew increasingly cold and the chances of catching the perp were reduced exponentially. While techs collected little pieces of glass and others dusted every surface for usable prints, the two detectives began their investigation. They were spared the chore of informing the next of kin about the death of their loved one. Their captain had prevailed upon his counterpart in rank back in Baltimore to pay the new widow the courtesy of an in-person notification.

The Senator's cell phone and his laptop computer were bagged and taken back to the precinct along with other pieces of this puzzle. Security footage from the building's elevator and outside cameras was also commandeered. When the forensic team couldn't locate the top and neck of the liquor bottle, patrolmen were sent outside to check dumpsters and under bushes for the missing piece. At least those cops were successful in moving the case along. The dumpster in the building two blocks up the street coughed up the evidence secreted in a knotted plastic grocery store sack. The neck of the bottle had been first wrapped in some very interesting and bloodstained computer printouts before it had been put into the bag. Now the detectives had their first lead, and his name was "Michael."

Chapter Seventeen

Since the partners had to wait for something to pop from the coroner and the forensic team, they proceeded to Capitol Hill to speak with Senator Abrams' colleagues as their first order of business. They actually had to briefly twiddle their thumbs in a hall while the whole bicameral Congress, consisting of both houses, observed a quiet moment of silence for their slain counterpart. Afterwards, when they talked with individual senators, the respectfulness proved to be very superficial because none had a good word to say about the guy from Maryland.

"Abrams was a real son of a bitch, so of course he had a lot of enemies," the senator from Wisconsin declared. "He had probably managed to piss off more people than Trump ever dreamed of doing even with 'the Donald's' twitter account spewing out venom."

An old senator from Georgia also pontificated. "I'm not surprised that Abrams met his end the way that he did. That piece of shit was as shifty as a polecat and stank just as bad. Somebody did a public service and should be commended for their efforts."

"He was as crooked as a desert sidewinder and just about as lethal," an Arizona representative chimed in. "So, I say good riddance to bad rubbish."

And so it went for the better part of the day. There were 535 members of Congress, and Jesse and Attiq concluded that perhaps, for the first time in recent history, those members might actually agree on something. The detectives then went back to the precinct to check for any new results on that end.

The coroner had placed the Abrams' case at the top of his to-do list, and confirmed his findings from the scene after the in-depth autopsy. The senator had quickly bled out from a fatal wound. He had perished between 7 and 9 pm on the previous night. The top of the Scotch bottle that was found in the dumpster matched the entry wound perfectly, and the physician had stated that if the neck of the bottle had been held like the handle of a knife, it made a perfect killing weapon.

Unfortunately, there were no prints on the neck of the bottle. It had been washed clean so not even a trace of the Senator's blood was left behind. Forensics did, however, match the blood on the computer paper that was wrapped around the bottle remnant to that of the Senator. Those pages had to have been nearby when the blood started to fly, and the smudged droplets seemed to support the theory that they were cast off during the deadly assault.

Technical wizards were now trying to trace the origin of those emails sent to Jason and Justin Abrams' computers at their college. After obtaining the proper invasive warrant, the sons' laptops were examined by the DC techs after they had been quickly confiscated by the authorities in Connecticut and couriered to Washington. Being hands on had not helped one iota. Whoever had sent the messages knew what they were doing and rerouted them around the globe from Buenos Aires to Lichtenstein and back via Indonesia and the Caribbean. So, to put it in layman's terms, the DC geeks had zip.

Jesse and Attiq read and reread the college emails. The actual substance and tone of the missives found in the trash seemed to strongly suggest that the dead Senator was being steadily blackmailed for one of his past misdeeds. When the sons' cache of old emails was finally scrutinized, the reason for the extortion soon became very clear, and it was a doozie right out of a soap opera. It wasn't that it was a very unique tale. That kind of thing probably happened a lot, but probably not to someone with so much to lose if the information that he was a cad as well as a deadbeat father was made public.

When the senator's own laptop was dissected, not one blackmail threat was in sight. There was plenty of hardcore porn on the MacBook Pro, and a massive amount of word product from the Senator's position on the Senate Budget Committee, but not a peep from this mysterious "Michael." So, the detectives came up empty-handed figuring out who the illegitimate son was who worked his scam through the two legitimate ones. The rest of the emails that still remained on the senator's laptop were innocuous. Perhaps government officials had learned a cautionary lesson after Hillary Clinton's faux pas.

Next, they examined the dead man's phone. There were plenty of recent messages left on it. The last several voicemails and text messages had come from his wife starting at 3:00 am Any previous ones had been deleted. The investigators would get another warrant for the call logs that went back further in time.

Now that Jesse and Attiq had a window for the time of death, the detectives began to watch camera footage from a little before 7 pm to a bit after 9 pm the previous evening. Because of the high-profile nature of the case, they were afforded plenty of additional eyes to watch frame after frame of images from both cameras. As each unidentified person came into view, more ancillary staff were tasked with matching the faces to actual residents of the building. They were searching for someone who didn't have a plausible reason for being there. Eventually, they narrowed it down to just four persons of interest who didn't seem to be a bona fide condominium owner.

It was easy enough to track down a bike messenger who had entered the building a little before 7:30 pm. He hadn't remained inside long, and left a few minutes later. His light-colored spandex outfit didn't appear to have any blood on it, and was too tight to conceal a bag containing the liquor bottle evidence. After checking the logs of all the messenger agencies that serviced the Dupont Circle area, they had a name—Keith Howard. He was a young college student on scholarship at American University, and he supplemented his almost non-existent income by working part-time as a bike messenger. He had a legitimate reason for entering and leaving the high-rise condominium. A lawyer on the sixth floor had verified that the young man had delivered important documents to him the evening of the Senator's murder.

The building's own night supervisor was actually helpful in identifying another person—a thirty-something blond woman who was also seen entering the building during the right time frame.

"That's Mrs. Schwartz's granddaughter. The old lady lives on the second floor and she's not in the best of health. So, Maddie stops by every Monday and Thursday like clockwork to check on her."

Frail, old Mrs. Schwartz corroborated her granddaughter's whereabouts and said that the young woman had stayed until after the 11 o'clock news was over before leaving.

Two down and two to go was the current tally. A short, well-dressed man with a rolling type of attaché case entered the building at precisely 7:30 pm. He was not seen leaving in the designated time frame. So, Attiq and Jesse canvassed door to door with his picture as well as that of a tall, dark-haired man who appeared to be in his thirties. That man was clad in a long black overcoat, and he had arrived a few minutes after 8 pm. He was seen leaving the building just fifteen minutes later. The two unknown male visitors were the last of their unidentified suspects.

The dogged detectives hit pay dirt on the fifth floor. A middle-aged couple, both curators at the Smithsonian, identified the man with the rolling little suitcase.

"Oh, that's Reginald," the wife informed them. "His full name is Reginald Cartier and he's an interior decorator with a very prestigious design company. He's such a dear to work with, and he goes the extra mile to make his clients happy. He actually was bringing us samples of upholstery and valence materials last night. We simply couldn't decide, and it took us forever to make our choices. Poor Reggie was stuck with us indecisive old fuddy duddies until after 10 pm."

"How about this man?" Attiq asked. "Do you know him, or have you seen him before?"

Both people shook their heads, but the lady of the house had a bit more to say that made her husband execute an impressive eye roll.

"He's very, very handsome," she simpered coquettishly, "so I definitely would recall that face if I had seen it. Does he perhaps live here on another floor and I have simply missed running into him?"

"Not to our knowledge, ma'am," Jesse answered while trying to keep a straight face.

The two detectives had no luck with the condo owners on either side of Abrams' unit. The couple to the right was on a Mediterranean cruise for the last two weeks. However, the other homeowner, an investment broker, opened his door and stared at them blandly.

"I suppose this has something to do with the circus going on next door—am I right?" he said resignedly. "I've already told a patrolman that I barely knew Jarod Abrams and I can't add any insights into your investigation."

"Sir," Jesse reminded him, "you and Senator Abrams have been next door neighbors for over five years. What can you tell us about him?"

"Absolutely nothing, Detective. Obviously, I knew that he lived in the condo next to mine, but we never really spoke. You learn to keep your nose out of other people's business, especially in this town."

"You never spoke?" Attiq wasn't buying that.

The investment broker sighed. "Gentleman, let me explain a fact of life. Washington DC is really a transient town, I'm afraid. People come, and people go, usually depending on the outcome of the next election. I have lived here for fifteen years and have had three adjacent neighbors during that time frame. Abrams was just the last one in the little parade. I'm not especially fond of bureaucrats, so I simply don't make an effort to be neighborly, and the Senator never came knocking on my door to borrow a cup of sugar."

The man with a social phobia and a desire for solitude denied recognizing the last unknown face when the detectives held up that photo. He then firmly closed his door in theirs.

Jesse and Attiq soldiered onward and upward. However, by the time that they had reached the ninth and final floor, they were getting discouraged. But then, they suddenly hit on another lead—gossamer thin—but a lead nonetheless. The older gentleman in the penthouse confirmed that he had ridden up in the elevator early last evening with the man in question.

"Are you sure this is the man?" the detectives asked again.

"I am, gentleman. We were the only two people in the elevator at the time. We didn't speak, but we turned to nod politely at each other. He got off before I did, of course, because this penthouse comprises the whole of the ninth floor."

"What do you mean by 'of course'? Did he possibly get off on the eighth floor—the one just below you?" Jesse asked anxiously.

"Of course it was the eighth floor, gentleman, one level down from me, and the very same floor as poor Senator Abrams."

Chapter Eighteen

So, now this unknown dark-haired man became "*the* person of interest" that they needed to find. However, in this bustling metropolitan city that had 680,000 indigenous residents as well as 22 million visitors a year, that definitely wasn't going to be easy.

Of course, this high-profile murder was really big news in the District and people hungered for details. Jesse and Attiq were constantly accosted by rudely aggressive and intrusive reporters everywhere they went, but they just kept uttering the same response to the probing questions.

"The investigation is still in its early stages and we have nothing that we can share with you at this time."

By day two of the investigation, the fingerprint evidence was starting to filter in. So far, only a few prints had been matched to names. Of course, most were those of the Senator, and the specialists were next able to match another set to his weekly cleaning lady by comparing them to her immigration application. Mrs. Abrams was also fingerprinted so that her's could be eliminated. Unfortunately, they most definitely did not correspond to an almost perfect full set lifted from the bed's headboard. In fact, those little beauties came back as belonging to a female lobbyist representing the National Education System. They were on file with the FBI because she had once taught in a public school.

The forensic criminologists were still diligently working on reconstructing the Scotch bottle, but it was like trying to put Humpty-Dumpty back together again. Finally, using an out-of-the-box approach, the innovation scientists bought an identical bottle of the same brand of liquor and added plaster of paris to replace the actual alcoholic contents inside. After the substance had hardened, they broke the glass around it and were tediously gluing pieces of a shard puzzle onto its surface.

Later that night, the determined team had their mosaic as intact as it would ever be. It enabled them to lift a clear print of an index finger and thumb from the middle of the bottle, and the detectives eagerly ran it through the national database hoping to get a hit. Suddenly, Jesse Cormier and Attiq Kabli had an identity for their suspect. How coincidental that his first name was "Michael."

Like bird dogs on the scent, the two men eagerly read every last detail that was on file about "Michael Wyatt." Apparently, he had been arrested and indicted over fifteen years ago in Baltimore, Maryland for numerous federal charges stemming from the operation of his import/export enterprise in the same city. That's why his prints were in the system. He was tried by a jury of his peers but found not guilty after a lengthy trial. Soon afterward, the exonerated man seemed to disappear from the scene and hadn't poked his head up since.

Attiq, who always liked to look for clues in the little details, pored over every document pertaining to that trial. Suddenly, he gave a gleeful fist pump and uttered a forceful "Yes!" when he found the connection. Jesse looked up at his partner in anticipation.

"I'll bet you'll never guess who defended Michael Wyatt in court over fifteen years ago. Come on, Jesse, guess! You shouldn't need more than one stab at this to win the prize!"

"Hmmm. Dare I guess the recently departed Senator Jarod Abrams was his attorney back then?" Jesse said as he waggled his eyebrows.

"Give the man a prize!" Attiq crowed.

"But this report says that Michael Wyatt suddenly seemed to evaporate into thin air soon after that all ended," Attiq added.

"Well, that seems a mite peculiar to me, and it just might lead a cynical person to believe that he may now be gadding about under another name," Jesse said thoughtfully.

"Who actually says *'gadding about'* in their everyday speech?" Attiq wanted to know. "Please don't tell me that you're next going to be referring to our suspect as *'a gentleman caller?'*" he teased his counterpart.

"You must accept me as I am, Partner, with all my little quirks and foibles innocently acquired in my humble and parochial Southern upbringing," Jesse answered as he played the role of a bumpkin. "Now, let's get serious and use that *new-fangled* facial recognition software to maybe get a hit on who he is now."

When that system was activated, it wasn't long before the detectives' computer screens were suddenly filled with a cascade of images. It was definitely the unidentified man from those camera images who was staring back at them, but his last name had changed from "Wyatt" to "Devereaux." The original Michael Wyatt and the Devereaux doppelganger were one and the same. However, it was Devereaux's face that was found on a current United States passport, on a California driver's license, on a pilot's license for a Learjet, and even on the cover of an old "Architectural Digest" magazine. To tie everything up in a neat little bow, his photo ID had been used to get a luxury rental car at National Airport on the day of the murder. More damning was the fact that his driver's license photo also appeared on a traffic citation issued on the night of the murder just two blocks from the scene. That had occurred well within the timeframe of the crime.

"It just keeps getting better and better," Jesse smiled in satisfaction.

"Yep, it's looking real good," Attiq agreed. "However, I think that we'll need to trace his rental car's trip log to find out exactly what he's been doing since Monday night. We can use backdated traffic cam footage to see where he went. This whole thing might not be all cut and dried. It could be part of some bigger plot."

"Sure, we can do that to cover our asses, but, right now, I think we've got ourselves a keeper," Jesse said with a satisfied smirk.

"Well, maybe not for long," Attiq advised his partner as he stared at his own computer screen. "Devereaux just turned that rental car in a few hours ago at the Baltimore/Washington Airport, and he has a plane ticket booked in his name for San Francisco leaving at …" suddenly Attiq looked stricken.

"What?" Jesse demanded.

"Our suspect is already wheels up and winging his way across the continent as we speak. Damn it, now we'll have to prevail on our brothers in blue on the Pacific end to detain him when he lands," Attiq said sorrowfully. "Somehow it doesn't seem fair that we did all the legwork, and somebody else is gonna get all the glory."

"No," Jesse agreed with a frown, "it just doesn't compute at all!"

Chapter Nineteen

Lawrence Buchanan was seated across the chipped and dirty Formica table from Michael at the San Francisco Jail, and he was beyond agitated and very demanding.

"What in the hell really happened in Washington, Michael? They're saying that you murdered a United States senator, for God's sake! Is that true—did you kill that man?"

Michael appreciated Lawrence's stunned incredulousness, but not the question.

"Isn't it in a law book somewhere that a defense attorney is never supposed to come right out and ask his client that very question?" Michael responded.

"I'm not some run-of-the-mill defense attorney, you idiot," Lawrence hissed. "I'm your brother-in-law!"

Michael heaved a sigh. "No, Lawrence, I did not kill Senator Jarod Abrams. Happy now?"

"Oh, no, Michael, I am far from happy. How did you even come to be in the same city with that man? I was informed that there is tangible and irrefutable evidence that you were not only in the same city, but actually in the same room with him on the night of his death. And then, two days later, there you are nonchalantly winging your way home to my sister like nothing had happened."

Michael chose to ignore Lawrence's ranting. "How is Amy holding up?" he asked quietly.

"How do you think?" Lawrence answered. "I always knew that you had a convoluted, sinister past, but did she know about it?"

"Amy knows everything about me, warts and all," Michael reassured him.

"So, she was aware that you went to Washington to see this senator?"

"Yes, we discussed it before I left," Michael answered his brother-in-law truthfully.

Lawrence's eyes narrowed. "My sister can be tight-lipped when she sets her mind to it, but she's also very smart and perceptive. Of course, the senator's murder was front page news out here, so Amy may have had an inkling of what might happen when you returned. Now it makes sense that she asked me to go with her to pick you up at the airport. How could you put her through that!"

Michael ignored the question. "After you're done having your tantrum, Lawrence, can you get her in to see me?" he asked.

The attorney shook his head. "I doubt that even I can work that kind of miracle, Michael. This is a high-profile federal case. You're up for arraignment later this afternoon, and there's no way that you'll be released on bail. The Washington DC politicos are champing at the bit to have you extradited back to their playground asap. I'm not licensed to practice law in DC, but I've put out some feelers to old law school contacts, so hopefully we can retain a decent defense attorney for you."

"Amy will know who to call," Michael quickly reassured his brother-in-law, "but just make sure that she does that from a burner phone."

Lawrence rolled his eyes and snorted, "Now why does that caveat not surprise me? Look, dear pain in the ass brother-in-law, just plead 'not guilty' when you are arraigned, and not one word more. Now, is there anything else that I should know before we waltz out onto that dance floor later this afternoon, or anything within reason that I can do for you in the meantime?"

"Just take care of Amy and the kids," Michael begged.

"That's a given!" Lawrence vowed.

~~~~~~~~~

Later that day, a protective brother went to pick up his sister from the quaint house on Steiner Street to take her to the arraignment. He was just about to tell Amy of Michael's request when she preempted him by asking that he make a quick stop at a Walmart. He must have looked bewildered because she quickly explained that she needed to buy a prepaid burner phone.

Lawrence knew that he really shouldn't have been the least bit surprised. Amy was always in sync with her husband, just as she had probably been since the day that they fell in love. Their marriage was like a storybook romance from the start. A worried brother sincerely hoped that this fairytale would have a happy ending, but he truly had his doubts.

Of course, the impaneled Grand Jury quickly handed down an indictment for first-degree murder to which Michael pled "not guilty." As Lawrence predicted, he was denied bail, and the next day the US Marshals would be escorting him back to the District of Columbia to eventually stand trial. Before he was led from the courtroom, he turned to see Amy staring back at him. Her bright eyes looked determined and she mouthed, "I love you." Looking equally supportive, Tom Buchanan, his father-in-law, pumped a clenched fist and winked as if to say, "Hang tight, boy, we're behind you." Monica Buchanan simply smiled worriedly.

On the way home accompanied by her brother and mother, Amy turned to Lawrence.

"Drop me off downtown at Fisherman's Wharf, please. I'll uber my way home later."

Her brother looked flabbergasted. "Now why in the hell do you want to go there, Amy? People will recognize your face because this whole fiasco with Michael is all over the news and the scandal sheets. People might start accosting you and asking questions, or maybe they'll be downright rude and offensive."

"Just do as your sister asks," Monica Buchanan's voice said forcefully from the backseat.

Ever obedient to his mother's wishes, Lawrence coasted to a stop near Pier 39 at the edge of Fisherman's Wharf. As Amy slid from the front seat and put on a big floppy hat and huge sunglasses, her mother sought to reassure her daughter.

"Your father and I will stay with Amelia and the children until you get home, Darling. Do whatever it is that needs to be done. We'll be holding down the fort, so take your time. We'll be waiting for you."

Amy smiled tremulously and began walking away. She looked more like a young Audrey Hepburn strolling the streets of Rome rather than a frightened wife whose husband was accused of murder. When she had enmeshed herself in the teeming masses of tourists, she took out the burner phone that she had purchased earlier with cash. She reached Sam Spade on the first ring and brought him up to speed. Michael's friend assured her that he would set things in motion on his end.

Now that she had done all that she could do, Amy walked aimlessly until her feet ached. Finally, she found an empty bench that faced the Bay. It was a clear day and she could see old Alcatraz prison in the distance. Long abandoned as a penitentiary, it was now in crumbling ruins just like Michael's life and her own. At that moment, Amy felt the hatred swell in her chest for the man who had been Jarod Abrams. Then she began to cry.

Chapter Twenty

Just as Lawrence Buchanan had foretold, the US Marshals escorted a shackled Michael to the airport the next day. They were the first to board the jumbo jet with their prisoner between them, and they sat in the very last row of the plane until it touched down in DC. Having arrived at their destination, the trio was the last to leave, and their ultimate stop was the Second District Metro Police Department where Michael was photographed, fingerprinted, and processed into the system.

The incarcerated man was finally taken to a claustrophobic, windowless room where he was handcuffed to a steel ring in the center of another scarred table. Thanks to Amy's alert, Sam had arranged for Manus Kirshner and Ellis Faraday to be on hand, and the two men were now bracketing Michael like bookends. Both attorneys were licensed to practice law in the District of Columbia, and they planned to vigorously protect the rights of their latest client. After an in-depth private discussion with the accused man, Ellis Faraday opened the door and beckoned to the two detectives lounging in the hall.

"Although he is under absolutely no obligation to do so, Mr. Devereaux has agreed to talk with you in an effort to clarify certain things regarding this travesty, and to reassure you that you have arrested the wrong person for this murder. Of course, either I or my learned associate counsel, Mr. Kirshner, may jump in from time to time to prudently caution our client not to answer a particular question if we feel that you are perhaps overstepping the bounds of a reasonable and unbiased interrogation."

Attiq Kabli and Jesse Cormier then walked slowly into the fluorescent-lit room. Attiq took a folding chair that faced Michael across the table, while Jesse nonchalantly leaned against a wall off to the right. The dark-skinned detective had several glossy 8 x 10 pictures in his hands that he carefully placed before him. He plucked the top photo from the stack and gently laid it down between himself and the prisoner. It looked gory and gruesome and certainly was not for the faint of heart.

"From emails we have read, we know Senator Abrams was your father, and this is a photo of his corpse, Mr. Devereaux," Attiq explained unnecessarily. "That's exactly how we found him in the kitchen of his own apartment. Want to tell me how the Senator managed to wind up in that condition?"

Michael stared into the interrogator's dark eyes. "I have no idea. When I left him, he was alive, intact, and breathing."

Attiq snorted. "Well, at least you're willing to admit that you were in the same room with him that night. It would be stupid to do otherwise because we have a solid eyewitness who saw you get off the elevator on your father's floor right before he was killed. We also have you on various cameras going into the building as well as in the elevator. And let's not forget that you were logged in by a traffic cop when he wrote you a moving violation just two blocks from the crime scene. And, last but not least, we have your prints on the murder weapon," Attiq concluded triumphantly.

"Excuse me, Detective," Manus interrupted, "but I'm an old man who is sometimes forgetful. However, I really thought that I heard that the neck of a Scotch bottle was determined by your coroner to be the actual murder weapon. And, I also heard that there were no fingerprints on it. Please correct me if I'm wrong."

Attiq lifted an eyebrow and replied evenly as he ignored the attorney and stared steadily at Michael.

"The neck of that Scotch bottle was actually washed with dish detergent before it was wrapped in some very damning computer printouts and discarded in a dumpster very close to where that traffic cop pulled you over, Mr. Devereaux. However, we do have very clear prints of your thumb and index finger on the glass body of that bottle. How do you explain that? Are you going to say that you were in the midst of sharing a drink with your old man before this all went down?"

Michael matched the detective with his own stare.

"No, we were not sharing a drink. I had merely picked up the bottle to read the label."

"Okay," Attiq continued, "so I am going to assume that this wasn't exactly a social visit and that your father was intending to drink alone."

"I have no idea what he was intending to do with the rest of his evening," Michael answered. "I came to say what I had to say to him, and afterward, I left him to his own devices."

Attiq actually smiled a predatory little smirk. "I'm going to go out on a limb here, and venture a guess that this little reunion wasn't actually all warm and fuzzy for either one of you. Senator Abrams had extensive redness and swelling on his left cheekbone, and, when you were taken into custody, your right hand was photographed. You had some impressive bruising and swelling as well."

Ellis Faraday chimed in at this point. "Detective, surely it is beyond your forensic scientists' commendable capabilities to declare a definite match for bruises on cheekbones and boo boos on someone's knuckles. I applaud them if they can state, unequivocally, that those two injuries are a match."

83

Attiq again ignored the attorney and kept probing. "I don't think this was anything even close to an amicable meeting, but I'll let that go for a minute. If you are so anxious to be forthcoming, why don't you tell me why you came all the way from San Francisco, California to see Senator Abrams here in Washington? What was so imperative that you felt the need to speak to him in person?"

"I heard that he was the one seeking me out, not the other way around," Michael answered.

"Who told you that? How did you first come to hear of it?" Attiq wanted to know.

Manus was quick to interject himself into the conversation. He was quite wily and knew just how to turn a phrase to mislead interrogators without actually lying.

"Michael and I discussed it. I made him aware that Senator Abrams had come to my office and was asking about his whereabouts."

Now Attiq actually did address Manus. "So, you were the first to tell Mr. Devereaux of Senator Abrams' desire to find him, and you knew Mr. Devereaux's whereabouts even though he was going under an assumed name?"

Manus merely shrugged his shoulders and his answer was a deflection.

"Michael always has been a client of mine. And, just let me add that it is not against the law for a person to change his name. Movie stars do it all the time. Did you know that John Wayne's birth name was actually Marion Morrison or that Michael Caine was really christened Maurice Micklewhite?"

Attiq ignored the old attorney once again and persisted with a questioning look.

"Why did you decide to become Michael Devereaux right after your alter-ego, Michael Wyatt, had stood trial on a litany of federal charges in Baltimore?"

Michael looked at his interrogator calmly. "I wanted a fresh start in a different place where people weren't always going to be remembering that I was once falsely accused of crimes that I hadn't committed. Even though I was acquitted of all the charges, people would still remember the ugly gossip and innuendo."

"We have done our research and we know that your father actually defended you at your trial. Were you aware at that time that he was really your biological parent?" Attiq asked curiously.

"I have known that he was my father for over fifteen years, and, at the time, he knew that I knew," Michael answered truthfully.

"Is that why he defended you in court?"

Michael shrugged. "I would be speculating on what his thoughts were at the time. Perhaps his actions were a one-time attempt at doing the right thing. However, afterwards, we both felt that there was no longer any familial obligation on either side. We agreed to steer clear of the other, and we did just that until I heard that he was trying to find me."

"So, you weren't trying to blackmail him?" Attiq said as he next produced pictures of the bloodstained extortion emails.

Michael eyed them carefully. "These did not come from me," he stated forcefully.

"But the Senator did confront you with them, didn't he?" the detective insisted. "He had been steadily paying you off, thousands at a time. Was he finally saying enough was enough and that pissed you off?"

"Yes, he did show them to me, and I told him the same thing that I told you. I didn't send them. However, I do think that someone had come into the details of a long-buried past and was pretending to be me. I never told anyone of the fact that Abrams was my father because I swear to you that I wanted nothing to do with him. I didn't want either his money or his attention. I had a good life out on the west coast. I certainly wouldn't have wanted to revisit a painful past and stir up a hornet's nest."

"Exactly how did you come by the knowledge fifteen years ago that Senator Abrams was your biological father?" Attiq asked.

"The man who raised me actually knew the truth, but I wasn't made aware of the fact until his death," Michael answered truthfully.

"That would have been Philip Symington. Is that correct?" the interrogator asked for clarification.

Manus again stepped in. "Yes, Detective, that is correct. I can attest that Mr. Symington, also a long-time client, had given me a sealed letter to present to Michael upon his death. When I went over Philip's will, I gave Michael the letter. I am assuming that is when he learned of his parentage."

"So, you kept that very crucial bit of information to yourself, Mr. Devereaux? Are you saying that you never shared that knowledge with anyone, not even with your wife? That's pretty hard to believe."

"My wife never even heard Jarod Abrams' name until I told her about him before I came to see him last week," Michael insisted. "It's not exactly something that I was proud of and eager to share."

"So, over the years of your marriage, it never came up. Is that what you're saying?" Attiq said incredulously. "Are you sure that maybe the two of you didn't decide at some point that it was time for a little payback, and you started twisting the screws. Was your sympathetic wife complicit in your blackmail scheme?"

A look of anger was in the throes of transforming Michael's expression when Ellis Faraday broke in to put an end to an imminent explosion.

"You are going way out of bounds, Detective. If you persist in dragging an innocent woman into this discussion who is not here to defend herself, then my client is done being cooperative!"

Attiq changed tactics in an effort to keep the suspect off-balance and to shut his mouthpiece up temporarily.

"We know that you went to Baltimore after the murder, Mr. Devereaux. We are in the midst of getting street camera footage to see exactly where you were for the two following days and who you saw. Perhaps, there is more to this than a simple blackmail plot that got out of hand when you confronted your father. We know that your stepfather, if that's what you want to call Mr. Symington, had owned a business with questionable ties to the Mafia. How does that play into this scenario? Maybe they were the ones urging you to blackmail Abrams to further their agenda."

"Oh, for Pete's sake," Ellis interrupted, "first you accuse Michael of blackmail and murder, then you drag his innocent wife into the mess, and now it's the Mafia. You're clutching at straws, my friend, and being absurd. You might as well pull Freddie Kruger into the mix and we can have ourselves a real ghoul party!"

Chapter Twenty-One

Jesse, who had been silent up until this point, pushed himself off the wall, put his hands in his pockets, and began to stroll casually across the room behind his partner.

"Mr. Devereaux—Michael—I heard that you're a real family man," he began in his slow drawl. "Got yourself four young kids out there in San Francisco. Now that's real nice. I'll just bet that ya love 'em to death. I got two teenagers myself, and even though they might get on my last nerve from time to time, they mean the world to me. You see, I'm a good ole Southern boy, born and bred, in case my accent didn't give you a clue. And down in my neck of the woods, which would be Louisiana, we value family above everything. Denying your own flesh and blood—well, that just doesn't compute. It's downright abnormal and against the laws of nature. So, you see, I sure can understand how being abandoned by your Daddy can hurt really bad. It just ain't right. Stuff like that doesn't just go away. It's gonna fester deep down under the surface and eat away at your insides."

Michael realized that this seemingly amiable detective was going for the "good cop" role in this drama, so he remained silent as the man continued to speak as he paced.

"Now, me and my partner have been talking to a bunch of people about Jarod Abrams, and, to tell you the truth, we weren't getting a real good vibe about that man. No siree! In fact, almost everybody claimed that he was an ornery son of a bitch. It was always his way or the highway, and he never had the time to listen to anyone else's side of a story. So, I can understand if you tried to explain something to him and he just didn't want to give you the benefit of the doubt. So, just maybe, things got out of hand.

Now, my friend, the district attorney wants to go with a charge of premeditated murder, but I just can't get on board with that. If you had wanted to kill your father from the get-go, you would have brought a gun or a knife to do the deed. So, now I'm thinking this whole thing wasn't planned out beforehand. I do believe that what happened was unintended and what attorneys call a crime of passion. You argued, he pushed your buttons, and then suddenly both of you were way past spitting mad. It escalated, the fists flew, and you grabbed the first thing that was handy because you felt threatened. That's only natural. If we want to call this crime anything, I personally think that this situation was more manslaughter rather than cold-blooded murder. If you tell us exactly how it went down, maybe we can put in a good word with the district attorney."

Michael didn't need to answer because Ellis Faraday was suddenly laughing loudly.

"My, my Detective, you are extremely entertaining with your charming rendition of a country yokel. You ought to take your show on the road and do the dinner theater circuit. Paying customers could then enjoy rubber chicken along with lots of your baloney. To be accurate, it's a fact that you have absolutely no clout with the judicial system and never will in your capacities as homicide detectives. Your mandate is to investigate and document all of the evidence pertaining to a crime. Unfortunately, you have been derelict in your duty because you haven't unearthed everything pertinent to this case. There is someone else involved.

Now, I do believe that this interview is over because it is quite obvious that you are already convinced of my client's guilt. That's very unfortunate because it means that the real blackmailer and murderer is still out there laughing his ass off because he has managed to pull the wool over your eyes. Take the blinders off, gentleman, and go back to the well once again. There is more evidence to be collected."

Attiq managed to have the last word in the discussion as Michael's two attorneys were preparing to leave the room.

"Mr. Faraday, we have this crime all wrapped up and tied with a big red bow. Your client had both the motive and the opportunity to commit it, and we have documented his part in the Senator's murder with substantial evidence to back up our conclusions. We don't have to second guess anything."

~~~~~~~~~~

Much later, after Michael had been transported to the Central Detention Facility at the District of Columbia Jail, Attiq and Jesse sat pondering the case.

"You know, Attiq," Jesse mused aloud, "maybe that slick lawyer is right. Maybe this whole case is just too neat and tidy with all of the little pieces falling nicely into place for us so that we could get the picture. When have we ever been able to close a murder of this magnitude so easily? I hate to say it, but everything that we've got so far is all circumstantial, and Devereaux's old Perry Mason lawyer might create reasonable doubt in the minds of the jury when it goes to trial. I mean, look at Michael Devereaux. He's handsome and clean cut and the epitome of a loving and devoted husband and father. Why would he chance jeopardizing any of that now?"

Attiq gave his partner a rather doleful look. "Just don't say it, Jesse. Please, do not trot out your favorite line of 'it just doesn't compute.'"

"But it doesn't—compute, that is," Jesse found himself arguing. "Devereaux is an extremely wealthy man in his own right out in San Francisco. His net worth is probably in the millions. Why would he suddenly, after over fifteen years, be hitting his old man up for dribs and drabs of $5,000 here, $10,000 there, and so on and so on. What would have been his motivation to put that into play at this late date? And why go through Abrams' other sons to get it moving? Those boys have admitted that they made their father aware of the first communication several months ago, so the Senator knew or suspected what was about to go down, and that's why he was looking for Devereaux to nip it in the bud."

"Okay," Attiq agreed, "so some things don't add up. Keep spit balling ideas, Jesse."

"Well," his counterpart obliged, "I am now asking myself why Devereaux didn't just confront the man himself instead of going through the college boys? Maybe the Senator never actually met with his blackmailer in person. Maybe he paid him off through an intermediary. Perhaps, if all of that had been done face to face, Abrams would have seen the identity of his nemesis and knew it was all a sham because it wasn't Michael Devereaux.

And, there's another thing that's still open-ended. Since I like all my ducks to line up in a neat little row, I've also been bothered by the fact that we can't match a pattern of cash withdrawals from any of Abrams' many bank accounts that correspond to the dates of the emails. Obviously, someone was paying the money, but who?"

Attiq looked thoughtful. "So, are you really buying into the possibility that Devereaux might be telling the truth when he said that the emails didn't come from him and that he wasn't the real blackmailer?"

"Maybe," Jesse admitted. "I'll play devil's advocate for a minute and say that someone else was playing the extortion game and it was never done up close and personal. If we are going to entertain that possibility, then we also have to find out how that unknown person knew of a familial connection from thirty-odd years ago."

"That means a little field trip to Baltimore," Attiq decided. "And while we're there, we can check out the places where Devereaux went and the people that he saw in the days following the murder. If somebody was in on the scam or had a dog in this fight, he might have met with them before he flew back to California."

Chapter Twenty-Two

The next day, after getting a thumbs up from their captain, Attiq and Jesse negotiated their way around the challenging Capitol Beltway until they could finally access Interstate 95 towards Baltimore. They had obtained all the printouts of Devereaux's rental car route as well as the stops he made in the following days. Their first destination would be the huge condominium complex of "Symington Place" in the heart of the city. Apparently, Devereaux had spent the night there on Monday.

Baltimore was a bustling little place with narrow downtown streets that were congested with traffic. The two detectives couldn't miss the various corner kiosks that were hawking the latest edition newspapers. Their lurid headlines were in bold print: "Spurned Love Child Takes His Revenge." The federal buildings in the Inner City were flying their flags at half-mast, and the courthouse entrance was adorned with black bunting.

"Sort of a dichotomy, if you ask me," Jesse remarked with a smirk.

"Oh, Partner, don't you know that's true of all politics. It's all about decorum and trying to keep up appearances," Attiq answered cynically.

Eventually, they flashed their badges at the gatehouse of the impressive Symington Place triple complex, and a call was made to the head of security. Sam was ready and waiting for them at the door to his office. Michael had asked Manus and Ellis to keep Sam in the loop about every piece of evidence that was made available to the defense attorneys in the discovery process, as well as the actions that were being taken to solidify the case against him. Therefore, Sam had made the necessary preparations and relished jerking these two clowns around a bit.

"Gentlemen, how can I help you today?" the old PI asked amiably.

"Are you Samuel Spade, the head of security here," Attiq wanted to clarify. "Is that correct, Sir?"

"Yep, that's me alright, but don't stand on ceremony. Just call me Sam."

Jesse found that he had to comment. "That's the same name as that private eye in those old movies that starred Humphrey Bogart."

"Is that a fact," Sam said in wonder. "I'm not much for old movies unless they're something that Clint Eastwood was in like 'Dirty Harry.' You gotta understand that I'm more of a sports nut, and I never miss an Orioles or a Ravens game on the tube. Now, I really can't stand the Pittsburgh Steelers, and that New England Patriot guy, Tom Brady, well, he's a real prima donna and I don't like him either."

Attiq tried to get the meandering man back on track.

"Sam, we were told that you're responsible for the security of this place and that you know all about the comings and goings of the residents as well as any of their visitors. We're investigating the murder of Senator Jarod Abrams and, at present, Michael Devereaux is our prime suspect. We just have to nail down a few loose ends. According to traffic cameras, Devereaux came here on the evening of the murder, and it seems as if he may have spent the night because his car didn't leave the premises until the next morning. He actually built this place many years ago, so it's possible that he still has ties to someone who lives here."

"You don't say," Sam replied as he scratched his head. "I always heard that Michael Wyatt built this establishment, so I guess what you're trying to say is that Michael Wyatt and Michael Devereaux are one in the same person. Do I have that right?"

"Yes, you do," Jesse answered this time in a patient tone of voice. "Do you know him?"

"Nah," Sam denied, "I've only been on this job for just a few years so that's all way before my time."

"That's okay," Jesse reassured Sam. "What we need from you is the sign-in log from the gatehouse on the night in question. We want to find out who Devereaux had come to see. Maybe you also have cameras inside the three adjacent buildings and in the elevators. Recordings during our time frame would be very helpful in narrowing down the list of residents."

Ever-eager Sam Spade suddenly looked crestfallen.

"Gosh, fellas, I only wish that I had known that you were coming sooner. All of our recording equipment gets erased after seventy-two hours, so whatever you wanted to look at is already long gone."

"You don't have backup storage?" Attiq asked in disbelief. "I would think that a swanky place like this would have all the bells and whistles."

Now Sam looked sheepish. "Well, we've had a bit of a glitch with that system and I haven't gotten around to getting it fixed. It's definitely on my to-do list; it just hasn't actually been done yet."

It took every bit of their willpower for the two detectives not to roll their eyes and sigh in frustration.

"So, okay," Jesse responded, "how about the physical sign-in sheet or log book. You can't mess up with an actual pen and paper."

"That's right," Sam said brightly, "you can't go wrong with that."

The wily PI then rummaged in a file cabinet for several minutes until he located the proper log ledger for the week in question. He carefully wet the tip of his finger and laboriously turned pages until he got to the proper day.

"Now what time are we talking about, guys?"

"Sometime after 9:00 or 9:30 pm.," Attiq supplied.

Sam was now shaking his head sadly. "Sorry, fellas, there's no Michael Wyatt or Michael Devereaux listed on the sign in log during that time frame. In fact, that name doesn't crop up anywhere at any time. Are you guys sure that you got the right day?"

"Yes, it's the right day," Attiq assured him. "That leads us to believe that someone may have agreed to open the gate for him without the formal identification process. Which of your employees was on duty that evening? We'll definitely want to talk with him or her."

Sam next pulled out a pair of thick wire-framed glasses and meticulously set about polishing them with the tail of his shirt. He then pulled another log book, held it close to his face and squinted.

"I'm real sorry, good buddies, but you've struck out again. The security employee listed on the main gate for that night is no longer with us. He was a new hire, but his gig only lasted a few nights before he up and quit with no notice."

"Did you even vet this man before you hired him?" Jesse asked with a frown.

"I was going to get around to it, but when he left so soon, it just didn't seem to matter a whole lot in the long run," Sam answered with a cavalier wave of his hand.

"Does that kind of thing happen often?" Attiq asked. "You know—here today, gone tomorrow."

Sam sighed theatrically. "Look, detectives, sitting in a tiny little gatehouse for eight hours isn't exactly an upscale white-collar job, you know. Truthfully, we don't usually have a line of eager applicants busting down our door for that golden opportunity. So, sometimes, you just have to take what you can get and make the best of it. We always have a warm body at the gate and that's what the residents want to see."

Attiq and Jesse looked at each other and grimaced.

"Can you at least tell us the name of this particular man who worked the gate that night?"

"Sure I can," Sam said happily. "His name was John Smith!"

As the disgruntled and stymied detectives left, Sam made a call to Duff.

"Incoming on the way!"

~~~~~~~~~

Even though the vehicular records showed that Devereaux had made his first stop the next morning at the downtown law offices of Kirshner and Faraday, it would have been useless for the Washington detectives to make an appearance there. Because of attorney/client privilege, the two lawyers would not be talking with the detectives about the case. So, instead Attiq programed the car's GPS to take them to the massive Symington & Son Import/Export building closer to the Inner Harbor.

While Sam Spade had appeared to be somewhat dim-witted and plodding, Vincent Duffinetti looked to be the epitome of sharp shrewdness.

"Of course, I know Michael," the Italian readily admitted. "I've known him since he was a wide-eyed kid that Philip Symington was raising."

"I'm curious," Jesse said slowly "Exactly how did that come about? I mean, it's really strange that we haven't been able to unearth any formal adoption papers that would have made old man Symington his legal parent."

"Well," Duff said with a shrug, "you'd have to ask Philip Symington how that came to be, but since he passed away years ago, I guess you'll never know."

"We think that perhaps you do have knowledge of those details, Mr. Duffinetti," Jesse taunted.

"Did you get that idea from your crystal ball, Detective, or from a fortune cookie?" Duff answered snidely.

"This might go a lot easier if you would cooperate, Sir," Attiq snapped. "What we do know for a fact is that upon his death, Mr. Symington named Michael Wyatt as the exclusive owner of this enterprise."

Duff looked at the two detectives as if they were stupid.

"Philip had no other family, so, of course, he made Michael his sole heir."

Attiq wasn't finished. "Be that as it may, a few years later things changed drastically. All of a sudden, Wyatt signed the whole business over to you and leaves town, changes his name, and puts 3,000 miles between you and him. Now why would he do that?"

"Again, I don't know his motivation and you'd have to ask him. Michael and I parted on the best of terms. We have kept in touch, so it wasn't unusual for him to stop by occasionally to see how the business was doing."

Jesse lobbed the next salvo. "We do know that Devereaux paid you a visit on the Tuesday after the murder went down. In fact, he came to your apartment on the harbor and actually spent the night," the detective said triumphantly.

"Of course, he did," Duff agreed, "and it certainly wasn't the first time that he has slept in our guest bedroom. My wife loves to spoil him during his infrequent visits, so she spends all day cooking his favorite meal."

"What did you talk about?" Jesse asked.

"To the best of my recollection, the conversation was mostly centered around his family and his architectural work out in San Francisco," Duff answered vaguely.

"He never mentioned that he had been to Washington and met with Senator Abrams?" Attiq asked point blank.

"No, he did not," Duff answered just as succinctly.

"Okay, so, did you perhaps discuss the fact that Senator Abrams was responsible for spearheading an FBI inquiry into the import/export business that you now own?" Jesse pushed.

"Gentleman," Duff heaved a disgusted sigh, "somebody is always conducting another witch hunt aimed at innocent law-abiding minorities. I really should think about filing a lawsuit that highlights the intrusive ethnic profiling and persecution of poor Italians just trying to make a living. The big boys in the federal government are all bullies who like making our lives miserable simply because they can."

"Sure," Jesse agreed. "You're pure as the driven snow."

"Exactly," Duff replied coldly.

~~~~~~~~~~~

"You know, this is getting us nowhere," Jesse groused when they left. "If we strike out at the last location, we're going back home with zip."

"Well, we're here in Baltimore now, so maybe the third time is going to be a charm," Attiq answered.

When the detectives located the final stopping place on Michael Devereaux's odyssey, they found it to be a busy local parking garage. When they walked out onto the street, they peered up at least three high-rise apartment buildings within a one-block radius.

"Well damn!" Jesse complained in disgust. "Devereaux could have gone into any one of these. Do we really want to go door to door with his picture for the next week or two?"

"I think that what we want to do is to go home," Attiq said morosely.

Chapter Twenty-Three

Later the next day, Sam was again sitting in David Parrish's apartment located in one of those same high-rise buildings that the two Washington detectives had given up trying to canvass. Of course, Michael was the topic of the evening.

"I just can't believe that Michael never told me that Jarod Abrams was his father," David said as he shook his head sadly. "If I had known that fact when he was just barely a pubescent kid living alone on the street, I could have done something about it. I could have made Abrams step up to the plate and take care of him, or at least see to his welfare."

"He didn't tell you because he had no idea who his father was back then, you doofus," Sam chided.

"Well, how did Philip Symington find out?" David said as he glowered at the mocking PI.

"Maybe he had someone investigate Michael's origins when he discovered a 15-year-old boy almost beaten to death in an alley by his house," Sam said innocently.

David narrowed his eyes as the light dawned. "It was *you* who dug down deep and found out the truth, wasn't it Sam? You always had a connection to Symington & Son, and it's not a stretch to think that the old man may have asked you to snoop around for him."

"I'm pleading the fifth on that one," Sam mumbled.

"But why didn't Symington tell Michael who his real father was when you found out the details?" David wanted to know. "Don't you think that it was cruel to keep that information from him?"

Sam huffed out a breath. "You didn't really know Michael back when he was just a boy, David. That kid didn't just have a chip on his shoulder. He had a damn boulder perched there. He made it clear to Philip Symington that he didn't want to know the truth because it was obvious that his biological father hadn't wanted him. Ergo, he didn't want anything to do with the man. When he was older, and after Philip passed away, I guess an adult version of Michael felt that he was strong enough to face the reality."

"That's really sad," David lamented. "He should have had a better life growing up."

"He *did* have a good life," Sam argued. "Philip Symington loved that kid and gave him a wonderful home. And Michael did everything that he could to make his mentor proud."

"Yeah," David said wryly, "and that entailed becoming a thief, a smuggler, and perhaps even a forger. The FBI had lots of suspicions back in the day, just not enough evidence to nail him."

"Do you regret not being able to arrest him when you were an FBI agent here in Baltimore?" Sam wanted to know.

"That's really too complicated for an easy answer," David replied. "I don't know how Michael and I managed to get so intertwined back then. Maybe we were just destined to have a strange, inexplicable connection, and sometimes you can't always figure out why your life take some really serpentine twists and turns. And now the beat goes on. He's gotten himself into another mess, a really bad one, and here we are wringing our hands and brainstorming how to come to the rescue."

"Yep, the beat does go on," Sam agreed. "And we've got to do everything in our power to help him get out from under whatever this thing is."

David looked pensive. "Sam, give me an honest answer. Do you think that Michael may have killed Jarod Abrams?"

Sam set his mouth in a grim line. "Look, David, if you're having second thoughts about helping to clear him, just say the word and I'm out the door. You're not in the detectives' crosshairs because nobody has made the connection between you and Michael. Play it safe, if you want, and go back to writing your little crime novels—no harm no foul. I'll do all the heavy lifting."

"You didn't answer my question, Sam," David said softly. "Both you and I know that Michael can be lethal if he feels that it is justified. He plays by his own set of morality rules. Do you think that's what happened last week in Abrams' apartment? Did the oily Senator set him off, and a vengeful neglected son suddenly decided that enough was enough?"

"Michael told me that he only talked with the Senator. He didn't say that he killed him in some fit of rage, so that's good enough for me," Sam declared. "Now, Mr. Doubting Thomas, are you in or are you out?"

"I'm in!" David finally declared with more certainty.

"Okay then, let's make a plan," Sam said. "The heart of this problem all started with some emails from a blackmailer. They didn't come from Michael, so our first order of business is to find out who else knew the identity of Michael's biological father. He certainly never told anyone, nor did I. Are you sure that no one in the FBI had a clue? You just said that the Feds investigated him pretty thoroughly."

"I was an ASAC or 'Assistant Special Agent in Charge' of the unit back then," David explained, "so I would have gotten any pertinent information. Of course, we weren't looking to find out who Michael's parents were. We were too busy trying to figure out exactly how he was running illicit things through his business."

103

"Well, it wouldn't hurt to revisit the issue," Sam mused. "You must still have some old contacts at the Baltimore FBI. Why don't you nose around a bit and see if there's anything there?"

So, David obliged. He showed up at the Woodlawn FBI office, got a visitor's pass, and then sought out some old colleagues who were still on the job. He explained that he was thinking of writing a new novel revolving around Senator Abrams. Was there any little tidbit of information that he could use to develop his plot that wasn't already out there in the media—maybe an earlier inkling that the Bureau had, way back in the past, that there was a familial connection between Michael Wyatt and Jarod Abrams?

Nobody took the bait and it seemed as if that was a dead end. Now it was back to the drawing board once again.

"Well, that narrows it down to the leak having come from Abrams' end," Sam said with a sigh. "That's a very big end, over a lot of years, in areas that we lowly peons certainly can't access."

David was also quite frustrated. "We certainly can't go anywhere near Abrams' family to ask if they knew of Michael without giving ourselves away."

"Somehow, I just can't picture the pompous and arrogant Senator suddenly feeling the need to unburden his soul to his family," Sam remarked. "He would have taken that secret, along with a ton of others, to his grave. Ironically, that's just what did happen."

"Okay, let's track this thing from a linear perspective," Sam continued doggedly. "We know exactly when Michael found out about his parentage, and I just may happen to know when he made Abrams aware of that fact. I believe he might have used that little bombshell as leverage when you guys were coming down on him with all your indictments. Abrams was in a private law practice at that time, and that would explain why he suddenly did an about face and decided to defend Michael in court."

"That makes sense," David agreed. "But what proof did he have to convince Abrams that he was the man's son?"

"I guess we'll have to ask him about that—well, maybe not us, personally," Sam explained. "We can't just waltz into the Washington jail as friends of an incarcerated man. Most likely, Michael's approved visitors' list only includes his immediate family and his attorneys. Amy has been staying in town and applies to see him as often as they'll allow, but I'm pretty sure those conversations are monitored and recorded. I'll speak to Manus and Ellis and they can get the scoop from Michael. Lawyer and client conversations are precluded from being recorded."

Chapter Twenty-Four

Michael was beginning the fourth week of his incarceration at the Central Detention Facility on D Street in the District of Columbia. The D.C. Jail housed adult males who were being detained while awaiting trial, and, at present, that population had swelled to over 2,000 inmates clad in baggy orange jumpsuits. That first day had been a scary and intimidating experience of walking through a narrow warren of cement floors with what could only be referred to as cages lining both sides. There were no classic iron bars. Instead, there were shiny grids of steel mesh that framed the entrance to claustrophobic alcoves barely big enough for one person, and certainly not for two. There was more steel inside the nooks — a set of bunk beds, a small sink, and a toilet bolted to the floor.

When the escorting guards stopped at Michael's new dorm room, it appeared to be home to another inmate as well. An African-American man eyed him passively as the restraints on Michael's wrists and ankles were removed and a thin pillow and some scratchy sheets were placed in his hands.

When Michael returned the man's stare and jerked a thumb to indicate the top bunk, his new roommate nodded and actually smiled showing lots of gold caps.

"I think you and me are gonna get along just fine," the man decreed with a dazzling grin.

That night Michael's bunkmate did some probing.

"Man, I heard that you actually offed some bigwig senator. Dude, that's impressive," he whispered.

"Well, maybe you shouldn't believe everything that you hear, my friend," Michael answered. "I'm innocent."

The man in the bunk below chuckled, "Aren't we all!"

It wasn't long before Michael heard other gossip as well. Apparently, if the prison grapevine was accurate, this inmate had caught his wife in bed with another man and, in a jealous rage, had sliced and diced both of them while they lay entwined in each other's arms. He claimed that his attorney was planning to offer a temporary insanity defense. In the meantime, Michael made sure to stay on his good side.

In the weeks that followed, Michael got the lay of the land in this little walled fiefdom. With a survivor's innate sense of self-preservation, he quickly learned the identities of the head honchos in all the little ethnic splinter groups that thrived throughout the prison. He managed to give them the respect that they thought was their due, and didn't cross any lines into their territory. He was also polite and deferential to the guards, never causing them any trouble. He simply kept his head down and didn't make any waves that would prove to be detrimental to his wellbeing.

Time, most assuredly, did not pass very quickly. Each day seemed to contain more than twenty-four hours, and the tedium and boredom were excruciating. At night, as he lay on his bunk, he stared up at the spiderweb of tiny cracks in the cement above his head and thought of his family. His sleep was fitful and filled with nebulous dreams in which he was lost in a maze and trying to find his way out. He could hear his wife and children calling to him, but, try as he might, he could never reach them. He would surge awake in a panicked state on the verge of hyperventilating.

At other times, he kept his clever mind active by imagining possible ways to escape. However, that was all a fantasy never destined to happen. The prison was a fortress, and it would take a miracle to get away with your skin still intact. Thus, in frustration, the depressed and lonely prisoner etched a parade of seemingly never-ending little tick marks on the wall beside his bunk.

Amy had insisted on staying in Washington, and religiously made appointments each week to talk with Michael via a monitor. That was how they would spend each brief 45-minute session—she was in an adjacent building and he was confined to a cubicle in another under a guard's suspicious eye. Both husband and wife knew that their conversations were far from private, so information was carefully cloaked in generalities and euphemisms.

"Your attorneys are working very hard on your case," Amy insisted, "and your *friends* believe in you, as well. They are doing everything in their power to prove your innocence," Amy told Michael over and over. "Now tell me how you are faring, my Darling?"

"I'd rather know how you are," her husband insisted. "And please tell me about the children."

"I'm fine and so are they, Michael. We're a strong bunch, and we hang tough when faced with something that threatens one of us."

"You shouldn't be stranded here week after week, Amy," Michael insisted. "Go home to the kids. They've lost a father and they shouldn't feel as if they've lost their mother as well."

"They have *not* lost their father!" Amy hissed. "Somehow, the real truth will eventually come out because very smart and persistent people are looking for answers. I have faith in them. I *know* that they will find the necessary evidence to clear you. And when the prosecutors and the jailers around here finally get a clue and release you from this place, it had better be with a very public apology. After that happens, you can come back to us. In the meantime, Mom, Dad, Amelia, and even my brother are all stepping in to keep life as normal as possible for our little tribe."

"I know that the older kids have heard the sordid details. How are they handling that?" Michael wanted to know.

"Philip has said that everything will get sorted out because 'Tonto' always has the Lone Ranger's back. Ella acts as if the allegations are a personal affront because her Daddy *always* does the 'right' thing! And the twins want you to know that 'Hamilton,' the hamster, needs a new name because he is a she who just had babies."

That bit of trivia actually made Michael smile. At least life continued to have some sense of normality when you were four-years-old and unaware of the harsh realities spinning their web around you. A father ached to see his children but was determined not to succumb to the temptation. He had managed to turn their lives upside down, and they needed to stay safely cocooned amongst the others in their extended family who would protect and comfort them.

If he were found guilty of this murder, best case scenario, he would be spending the rest of his own life behind bars three thousand miles away from them. Perhaps the twins would forget what their father looked like. Michael couldn't recall being four-years-old, so Jeremy and Daniel's memories would probably fade as time went on.

Michael's dilemma would be especially hard on serious and pensive Ella with her unwavering sense of right and wrong. She would never accept his unfair incarceration. Philip was sensitive as well, but he had proven that he was a survivor in the past when he was kidnapped. The boy-turned-adolescent was strong and would somehow survive this cataclysm, too, and move on. However, the question remained—how would Michael survive without all of them?

Amy and the children had been Michael's world for so long that he couldn't image another Thanksgiving, Christmas, or 4th of July celebration without being there beside them. His own childhood had been a hollow and sadly forlorn existence, but putting delight on the faces of his own children helped an adult father banish those memories to a locked compartment in his brain. Amy and the children provided meaning in what had been an empty void for him.

Maybe he had simply become too complacent and thought that this wonderful life would go on and on as the world continued to rotate on its axis. He had let his guard down, and now he had caused a lot of anguish and hurt. Guilt can eat away at you. Although Amy insisted that Sam and David were working on a promising lead, Michael suspected that Fate would not be that kind. A former criminal was finally going to be paying his dues for past sins. He hoped Amy would be capable of accepting the inevitable. She deserved so much better.

Chapter Twenty-Five

As requested, during one of their many private client/attorney sessions, Manus and Ellis had asked Michael how he had managed to convince Jarod Abrams of the paternity issue. Just as Sam had suspected, it occurred right before Michael was scheduled to stand trial on felony charges in Baltimore all those years ago. A young and slick wheeler-dealer had simply walked into the lawyer's inner sanctum one day, stated his claim, and backed it up with DNA left on a water tumbler. Michael said that he had no idea how Abrams had confirmed the match. During those years, his father had been in private legal practice, and Michael remembered the actual high-rise building facing the Inner Harbor and even the specific suite number.

"It was just a rather small operation at that point," Michael remembered, "because I think he was only biding his time awaiting the nod for a federal judgeship. He had a young secretary working with him named 'Lisa,' and also an older bookkeeper named 'Helen.' I never saw anyone else when I went there, which really wasn't that often. I think that the less that we saw of each other the better. After the trial was over, I sent him a check by mail and never saw the man again."

"Exactly how long had you known that Abrams was your biological father?" Ellis wanted to know.

"It wasn't until after Philip Symington's death. He had been privy to that information from the very beginning. He offered to tell me the details when I was fifteen, just days after he had taken me into his home. However, I was pretty hostile and angry at the time and I didn't want to know."

"And how did Mr. Symington find out the specifics of your origin?" Ellis pushed.

"I guess you'd have to ask Sam Spade about that," Michael equivocated.

~~~~~~~~~~

That was the exact question that David had now put to the old private investigator.

"You have to keep in mind that I was looking into Michael when he was fifteen years old," Sam explained. "Philip had supplied me with Michael's mother's name because that was a fact that the kid knew. Therefore, I just had to go back a decade and a half and investigate Jennifer Anderson. Even without Google in those days, it wasn't a hard thing to do. The next step consisted of tedious probing to find out where she had lived and who her parents were. When I found that information, I decided against confronting her family head-on because I doubted that Mom and Dad were very proud of the fact that they had set their daughter adrift when she became pregnant. Instead, I chose to do an end-run.

Jennifer had lived in Locust Point while growing up, and I made an assumption that she probably had attended the local high school. I confirmed that by digging up an old Kenwood High School yearbook and going through the pictures, one by one, until I found her. Then I made a list of other girls in her class and began tracking them down by using the school's Alumni Association. My story was that I was a PI trying to find poor Jennifer because her parents wished to have a long overdue reconciliation. Eventually, I hit the jackpot because one of those old high school chums remembered her and was willing to share.

"Sure, I knew Jenny," a local matron readily admitted. "She and I were never really close, but everyone knew her story. She was gossip fodder for months after it happened."

"What was the 'it' that happened," Sam asked trying to look perplexed and out of the loop.

"She got knocked up by some rich kid that she met on a school field trip to Fort McHenry. Poor Jen was infatuated and claimed that they were star-crossed lovers like Romeo and Juliet. She had this fantasy all worked out in her mind. They were going to elope to Elkton, Maryland and live happily ever after."

"But that didn't happen?" Sam had continued to probe.

"Oh, please! Jen was living in a dream world," her high school contemporary snorted. "She probably thought that if she wanted something bad enough, it was magically going to happen. That was just Jenny being Jenny—a dork with her head in the clouds. You can read all those fictional bodice-rippers that you want, but things don't happen like that in real life.

The asshole 'boyfriend' left her high and dry when he found out about her little 'problem,' and so did her stupid parents. If they want a reconciliation now, that's just guilt talking. Maybe they've finally decided that they want to meet their grand-child. Or maybe one of them has been told that they have a terminal illness and want to make amends before the Grim Reaper comes for his pound of flesh. In my opinion, they don't deserve to know where Jenny is."

Sam had been making progress, so he declined to make this woman aware of the fact that Jennifer Anderson had perished on a rough Baltimore street years ago after an overdose of illegal narcotics.

"Did you ever happen to meet this gutless cad of a guy who impregnated Jennifer?" he had asked with no guile in his tone.

"Well, I kinda remember him from the field trip," the young woman answered slowly, "and he was sort of handsome in a dark and brooding way. But after that, he and Jen always met away from school. I knew that his name was Jarod because Jen had it scrawled across her canvas loose-leaf binder with little hearts drawn all around it. I also knew that he was older than us—a senior at some hoity-toity private boys' academy in Greenspring Valley. Jen used to brag about that. She also boasted that he owned a red sports car with a vanity plate. I almost wanted to gag and throw up when she told us what it said—N-TITLED. Can you believe that? In my opinion, the jerk was just asking for somebody to key that car's fancy paint job if it ever parked in our neighborhood.

Anyway, I don't think there was a happy ending to Jen's pipedream. The last time that I saw her, she looked all down in the dumps, so I figured old Casanova had given her the heave-ho. I mean, let's get real. Why would a rich kid want to be shackled to a girl from the wrong side of the tracks who was pregnant to boot? The asshole probably gunned that sports car's big engine and drove away so fast that his mag wheels were throwing off sparks. It wasn't long after that when Jen dropped out of school. I heard that her parents were not very supportive. They actually 'disowned' her and locked her out of the house."

The woman blew out an exasperated breath. "You have to understand the way things were back during that time, Mr. Spade. People formed a hard and fast impression, right or wrong, that only loose, bad girls got pregnant before they were married. It was hypocritical thinking, but it was what it was. Young women got reputations and their parents shared in that shame. They usually sent their daughters away to hide in a home for unwed mothers until they had their dirty little secrets and gave them away for adoption.

Things are quite different today. Young teenagers become unwed mothers all the time and nobody bats an eye. Some high schools actually have childcare located right in the school to tend to the little ones during classes until their mothers get their diplomas. There are tons of social workers and state and federal agencies willing to lend a hand. Now, I personally think a lot of a certain kind of people take advantage of that and milk the system for all it's worth. More offspring from a number of different baby-daddies means more money in the mother's pocket."

Sam certainly didn't want to get into that philosophical quagmire, so he asked one last crucial question just to see how plugged in the woman was.

"Did you ever hear that Jennifer Anderson actually had her baby? Maybe she chose to have the pregnancy terminated?"

"That wasn't an option at that point in time," his contact assured him. "Jenny claimed that she was at least six months along when she left school in the beginning of February of that year. I remember that fact because she had volunteered to be on the Valentine's Day Dance committee and she left the other members high and dry when she disappeared."

Sam knew that Michael had been born in May, so that was no surprise. What he needed to nail down was the identity of the 'Jarod' who had been tooling around in his red chick magnet fifteen years ago. Luckily, he had an old buddy in the Baltimore Police Department who owed him a favor. The cop paid his debt by accessing the Maryland Department of Motor Vehicles records and unraveling the mystery. A classic red 'Triumph' sports car with the very unique vanity plate had once been titled to a young Jarod Abrams who had lived in Greenspring Valley, and who later went on to Yale to earn a degree in law.

"Okay," David said after he had heard Sam's methodology for slickly ferreting out the discrete details of the past. "Even though Jennifer Anderson's parents are long deceased, there still could be a lot of people who knew the story from years ago."

"Theoretically, there could be 1,500 *somebodies* who knew the real story," Sam informed him. "That was the number of students who were enrolled in that particular high school during Jennifer Anderson's days of matriculation."

"So," David mused, "*theoretically*, we have 1,500 suspects who could have gotten curious and found out the details back then. Maybe there were a few friends who were closer to Jennifer, and perhaps she felt comfortable confiding the name of her paramour to them. At this late date, there's just no way that we can track them down. Those teenage girls are middle-aged woman by now and most likely have married names. Anyone of them may have found themselves in a financial bind in present times and decided to become creative by cashing in on that deep, dark and secret knowledge. That's a helluva lots of suspects."

Sam wrinkled his forehead in deep thought. "But how did they know that Jennifer's baby was a boy that she named 'Michael?' No, 'Mr. Mystery Writer,' think it through. This is somebody with closer access to the facts. Not to mention that I've read those blackmail messages and I get the distinct gut feeling from the tone that they were written by a man."

Chapter Twenty-Six

David was again deep in thought. "I think that what you are hinting, my friend, in your less than tactful way, is that we have to start our search when Michael first confronted his father."

"Now we're on the same page," Sam crowed. "Try to keep up, please."

David cast his fellow sleuth a doleful frown. "Michael says that he doesn't know what lab Abrams used to confirm the paternity angle. Suppose we come at it from that perspective. Then the next logical step would be to find Abrams' secretary during that time because she might know which one it was, or maybe even the bookkeeper who may have been privy to that knowledge. Abrams might have put the lab work expense on his business debit sheet—you know, claim that he was simply following up for a client. If we can nail that down, we can investigate who may have had access to the medical results."

Yet again, there were long weeks of tedious digging into very old employment records before Michael's determined friends finally found the right two names. "Helen Davis," Abrams' bookkeeper when he was in private practice, was now in her seventies and had long since relocated to a Florida retirement community. However, "Lisa Wisniewski," the secretary, who was now Lisa Metcalf, was still in the area. David and Sam discovered that she was currently married and living in the Baltimore County suburb of Perry Hall. She worked as a Gal Friday for another attorney, a struggling personal injury lawyer with an office located nearby.

The two men waited patiently in the car early the next afternoon outside of a small office. At lunchtime, they saw a thin blonde woman matching her description leave the sorry-looking storefront building. This neighborhood was a far cry from the prestigious luxury space overlooking the Inner Harbor where she had once worked for Abrams. Since David and Sam had prudently decided that they didn't want to have their discussion in a law office, they then followed her to a nearby Burger King.

"Hello, Mrs. Metcalf," Sam said softly as he and David, without an invitation, abruptly sat down in the plastic seats across from the secretary. "My name is Sam and this man beside me held the position of an FBI Agent in the Baltimore field office during the time that you worked for Senator Jarod Abrams."

Sam didn't specifically mention that David was no longer an agent for the Bureau. He just threw that fact out there and let the startled woman draw her own conclusions. Hopefully, she might be a bit intimidated when they double-teamed her, and more motivated to be helpful.

"I worked for Jarod Abrams a really long time ago," the woman answered quickly.

"Yes, it certainly was quite a while back," David agreed, "but with the death of Senator Abrams, many old facts have suddenly become relevant to the investigation."

"But I thought that the man who killed him had been arrested. I even read in the paper that it was his own son," she said nervously.

"That's true at this juncture," Sam agreed, "however, we need to tie up some loose ends so that the case doesn't fall apart. All that we have now is completely circumstantial. You work for a lawyer, so you know how even the smallest little crack in the prosecution's presentation could have the whole

118

thing crash and burn. I'm sure that as a law-abiding citizen you wouldn't want that to happen because that would put a blackmailer and a murderer back on the streets."

"No, of course I definitely would not want that to happen," the woman murmured without meeting either of their eyes.

Sam and David exchanged knowing glances, and it was as if something telepathic had been communicated between them. This woman knew a lot, and it was probably going to take a certain amount of finesse to tease it out of her. Sam deferred to David to take the lead because the man could talk the talk and walk the walk of an influential proponent of law and order.

"What was it like working for Jarod Abrams back then?" David asked softly. "We've heard a ton of innuendo recently, both professional and personal, and most of it was .... well, let's just say that there wasn't a lot of admiration for the man. You can feel free to be completely open and honest with us. Our conversation is confidential, and it's not as if it would ever get back to a dead man or even his family."

"Well, he wasn't a very nice person," Lisa Metcalf finally whispered.

"As a boss or as a human being?" David wanted to know.

"Just any way you want to slice it," the former secretary clarified. "Jarod would trample over his mother's grave if he thought that it would give him a leg up to something that he wanted. He lied, and he used people all the time and then threw them away like yesterday's garbage when they were of no more use. He was deceitful, and you couldn't ever believe a word that came out of his mouth."

"We heard that he was a womanizer," David cast out his line. "Did you ever get a feel for that?"

Both Sam and David saw the deep, embarrassed blush that suddenly blossomed on the woman's neck and made its slow crawl up to her cheeks. Her head was now down, and she had her hands clasped tightly in her lap. This poor woman would make a terrible poker player.

"Jarod Abrams lied to you, didn't he?" David said gently. "He deceived you and then callously discarded you by the wayside when he grew tired of your love and devotion."

"I was very unsophisticated back then, Agent Parrish, and very naïve," Lisa Metcalf answered just as softly. "Jarod was very handsome and powerful, and that's like a turn-on to some women. I guess I was one of them. I was head over heels in love with a married man and knew that he would never divorce his wife for the likes of me. I was just content with any morsel that he threw me—an afternoon assignation in my apartment, even on the couch in his office on nights when we worked late. One weekend, when his wife was visiting their sons at summer camp, Jarod and I spent three glorious days at a lodge in the Berkshires. We never left the room. We just ordered room service for every meal. I was completely smitten and refused to listen to my more logical self. I must have known, deep down, that it would never last," she ended miserably.

"When did it end?" David wanted to know.

Now the jilted lover looked justifiably angry. "It abruptly stopped on a dime as soon as he won a seat in Congress. He had been leading me on the whole time during his campaign, swearing that he would take me along with him to Washington if he was successful in becoming a senator. That was all a bunch of lies. He simply packed up after the election and left me in the dust. The jerk wouldn't even write me a letter of reference for future jobs. I guess I was lucky that Helen, the bookkeeper, had already cut my weekly paycheck before he took a powder."

David tried to arrange his expression to display sympathy rather than abject pity. However, it was a ruse to find out just how forthcoming this woman would be with them.

"We've heard that the Senator left quite a lot of other people behind in his wake," the old FBI agent stated matter-of-factly. "Apparently, Michael Devereaux's mother was one of them. Did you ever meet Mr. Devereaux while you were working as Abrams' secretary?"

"I did when he became a client for a time," Lisa confirmed. "He was very nice and always polite, but he wasn't going by the name 'Devereaux' back in those days. He called himself Michael Wyatt, and he was well-known in the Baltimore community because he had built Symington Place down near the Harbor. He was very young and handsome, and looked so much like his father that it was uncanny. They had the same facial structure, the same blue eyes, and they even walked the same way. I'm surprised nobody seemed to notice at the time, but I'll bet that Mrs. Abrams would have. Michael Wyatt was the spitting image of her own two boys, Jason and Justin. I guess, just like everything else about Jarod Abrams, even his genes took precedence over everyone else's.

"So," David said pensively, "it seems that you knew they were father and son."

"I didn't know for sure," she answered. "I just surmised."

"What did it take to convince Abrams that Michael Wyatt was his offspring? I'm assuming that the Senator was skeptical at the time. He must have obtained some kind of proof, and that's why a biological father defended his own son in federal court down the road."

"I wouldn't know about that," Lisa Metcalf said succinctly. Although denying being aware of the means that Abrams had used to confirm paternity, the nervous, fidgety secretary was also again refusing to meet their eyes.

David and Sam exchanged perceptive glances once more, both on the same page for sure. Up until this point, the former paramour had been honest with them. However, now she was definitely lying, or, at the very least, intentionally leaving out crucial information. She must have had a good reason to do so, but they couldn't quite fathom exactly what it was. Short of using rubber hoses to beat it out of her, there was no way to get to the truth. Thus, for the moment, the two men silently rose and left Lisa Metcalf to her solitary Whopper meal.

Chapter Twenty-Seven

"I'm getting really bummed out by all these dead ends," Sam complained bitterly the next afternoon as he sat brainstorming with David in his condominium. "Michael's trial is just a few months away and we've got zip! That's a pretty pitiful state of affairs for a private investigator extraordinaire and a somewhat capable former Special Agent in Charge of the Baltimore FBI."

David glared but said nothing because Sam was right. They were still at square one, the clock was ticking, and the agent-turned-author was beyond frustrated by their lack of progress. He and Sam needed to somehow sort this out before it was too late because Michael was certainly counting on them. They had promised Amy that they were working on things from their end, and she had undoubtedly passed that thread of hope onto Michael. They just couldn't let him down.

David had always been capable of maintaining a steadfast focus, and he appreciated the PI's dogged tenacity as well. He was very aware that Michael and Sam had always been tight from the time that old Philip Symington had taken in the kid. David's relationship had developed much later, but it was no less intense. He and a now reformed criminal shared a strong affinity—a bond—for lack of a better word. It was almost preordained that they would always be there for one another when the chips were down. Not to mention, he couldn't let Michael take the fall for something he hadn't done. This time, there was too much at stake. Besides a loving wife, there were four young children who desperately needed a father back home where he belonged.

David heard Sam suddenly sigh theatrically. "I just have a real gut instinct that Lisa Metcalf, that legal secretary, knows something pertinent, but we can't badger her into telling us whatever it is that she's determined to hold back," Sam said miserably.

"Not unless you want the police to label us stalkers because the freaked-out lady suddenly decides we've overstepped our bounds and wants to take out a restraining order against us," David replied.

"So, okay, let's table her for a minute and concentrate on another aspect," Sam said. "Do you think that the Feds were being straight shooters when they claimed that they couldn't trace the origin of those various blackmail messages sent to the Abrams boys?"

David looked pensive. "Manus and Ellis got to look at all of the state's evidence during the discovery phase of Michael's future trial," he explained "They were also given copies of everything, so they're in possession of the local cops' report as well as the FBI's. Apparently, after all their dedicated effort, the tech wizards were stymied and said it was impossible to pinpoint anything. Whoever sent the messages knew his or her way around a computer because those emails seemed to be zinging through outer space before finally landing on a college laptop."

Suddenly, without any warning, a fevered light abruptly came on in Sam's eyes and he appeared to be in the throes of an "Aha!" moment.

"The word 'impossible' sounds very challenging," he said with a big grin. "Look, David, I've got to run because there's something I need to do right away."

"What's so important that it's suddenly got you all fired up?" David demanded to know.

"I've got to buy myself another burner phone," Sam called over his shoulder as he sailed out the door.

"And here I thought that we were supposed to be partners," David mumbled to the now empty room.

~~~~~~~~~~

Sam and David might be acting in concert to try to solve Michael's current problem, but there were certain prickly areas that were verboten for the one-time FBI agent. However, Sam's background as a former CIA operative had afforded him off-the-book and uber-clandestine avenues that he could travel when it was necessary to seek extraordinary help. That was the road that he was about to take.

The determined man quickly purchased an anonymous burner phone in a busy nearby convenience store and set about sending up a flare. There was a tedious protocol that Sam had to follow to the letter for this communication because the person whom he was contacting was beyond paranoid. Be that as it may, the recipient was also a very influential and intimidating genius who was well respected by the global spook community. Nobody seemed privy to the man's real identity. He was a pretentious and sometimes irritating little gnome who lived in London, and getting through the doors of his citadel was tricky. You had to be granted an audience, and only if he thought that you were worthy of his time.

Michael had met this weird little entity in person on two occasions, and Sam wasn't quite sure how to describe their relationship. The retired CIA agent had been a witness to the ongoing sniping and insults on both sides during Michael's interaction with the man whom he had come to call "Professor Plum." Therefore, it was iffy to speculate if this genius hacker would consent to aid his irritating antagonist. However, Sam was out of any other options to help Michael.

The old PI dredged up a specific IP address from memory that was only accessible on the Dark Web. He then sent a brief coded message stating that he was in dire need of a bit of assistance. Ten minutes later, he received the proper instructions to proceed. That entailed purchasing a certain rather arcane novel from a bookshop. This was the drill now in place once Sam had initiated contact. Although the titles of the novels varied, the old books were always by British authors, and this time was no different.

It took quite a few forays into musty antique bookshops until Sam located a novel by Thomas Hardy entitled "Jude the Obscure." The story had been originally published in 1895, and, although Sam had never read it, he scanned the back cover for a short synopsis. Somehow, someway, Professor Plum had become aware of the exact problem that Sam was bringing him because the chapters spanned the life of a man who had suffered throughout the years by facing difficult challenges.

Sam had his pick of codes and ciphers that he could employ to send his SOS message. Professor Plum would know them all and use his super computer to assist him so that he could get the actual text. Sam decided on the very old Vigenère cipher just to keep it interesting for a man who only agreed to take on problems if they were extremely challenging. In Sam's opinion, finding out the source of the blackmail demands fell into that category. Using keywords from the old manuscript, Sam explained what he needed, and stressed that time was of the essence. He promised that he would get copies of the emails from Michael's lawyers and forward them.

A mere half-hour later, a text was returned. It was terse and to the point: *"Already in possession of same. Have been following the drama, you nincompoop. Why wait so long to contact?!"*

The PI smiled. Well, that certainly sounded as if the weird little recluse had developed a soft spot for Michael and had been keeping tabs on his dilemma. Sam reckoned that stranger things had happened in the universe.

Chapter Twenty-Eight

After two days had passed, Sam received another text from a different source. Sam inferred from the strident words that David was beyond livid.

"Where have you gone? I know you're up to something. Either show up here or call me, damn it!!!"

Bright and early on the third day, the errant but not contrite private detective arrived on David's doorstep.

Bunny, David's wife, had just recently returned from the Baltimore Symphony's Austrian tour. She opened the door and gave her visitor a sad frown before placing a chaste kiss on the PI's cheek.

"The Master has summoned me," Sam intoned comically, "and being his lowly, humble servant, I hastened to obey my exalted Sire's wishes."

"He was worried, Sam," Bunny whispered, "and anxious and frustrated as well as a lot of other adjectives for being pissed at you because you went rogue on him. That's what you've done, right? You went off to handle things all by yourself. David doesn't like being in the dark and left out of the action."

Sam just gave her a crooked smile and a hug. "That trait probably harkens back to his days as an FBI drone. I guess it's time to face the music. Is the lion in his den just waiting to pounce?"

"Yep, that's pretty much where he's been since you left, and getting more and more agitated by the minute," the young woman answered wryly. "Call out if you need me to intervene during the flogging, and I'll try to rescue you from his cat-o-nine tails' wrath."

"You've been up to something!" were the first words out of David's mouth as Sam slowly sauntered into the spare room designated as David's work space.

"Perhaps," Sam answered nonchalantly as he made himself comfortable across the desk from his accuser.

"Do I want to know?" David now asked with his eyebrows raised.

"Probably best if you didn't," Sam shrugged. "We certainly wouldn't want to offend your moral sensibilities, now would we?"

"Stop speaking in the royal 'we,' you nitwit, and just tell me. I know whatever you've been doing was under the radar and probably illegal. I get that loud and clear even though you haven't said a word. For God's sake, man, just get with the program. It's not as if I'm going to rat you out to the cops!"

Sam usually wasn't one for gloating, but he couldn't help the Cheshire Cat smile that found its way to his lips.

"I found out the exact location where the extortion emails originated," he said with pride. "I'll betcha didn't see that coming, Mr. G-Man!"

"How?" was David's dumbfounded response.

"If I told you I'd have to kill you," Sam claimed with a bit of panache.

"Stop being a damn drama queen," David demanded, "and start sharing intel because I am not a patient man right now!"

"Isn't patience a virtue?" Sam asked with a quizzical look. "I know that I heard that somewhere. I guess that means that you're not very virtuous."

"Right now I'm teetering on being homicidal if you don't tell me what you know," David threatened.

Sam knew that he had pushed his schtick as far as he dared go with it. It was just so much fun to tweak David Parrish's nerves. However, the man was right. They were supposed to be working together. He needed to read the ex-FBI man into the operation. He would require his help to free Michael, so Sam got serious.

"I was given the exact coordinates via a very intellectually endowed source. From there, it was all about Google Earth. Take a wild guess who lives at that address—c'mon, guess!" Sam teased.

When David's expression did, indeed, take on a look of lethal intent, Sam hurried to supply the answer.

"Lisa Metcalf, Abrams' secretary from back in the day when he was in Baltimore—that's who resides at that address. We both knew that she was holding something back, and now we know exactly what that something was. Score one for gut instinct," Sam answered triumphantly.

David certainly didn't look convinced. "Are you trying to say that a middle-aged woman working as a secretary for a personal injury hustler managed to electronically evade the best technical minds in law enforcement? I think that's a bit of a stretch, Sam."

"Never underestimate the vindictiveness of an angry and scorned woman," Sam said smugly. "And just so you know, that sounded a bit chauvinistic, so I'd be careful saying things like that around your wife. You may find yourself kicked out of the marital bed if you persist in such disrespectful gender stereotyping."

David quickly held up his hands in the universal gesture of surrender as he glanced towards the kitchen where Bunny was brewing coffee.

"Okay, I'll admit that fifteen or so years ago, Lisa Metcalf had her suspicions about Abrams and Michael being father and son," David conceded. "She certainly could have used that ammunition as leverage when he became a senator and left her behind. She could have gone to his wife or the media to smear him during his campaign. She could have done a lot of things back then, including extorting him to keep quiet. Why did this thing suddenly evolve into blackmail now? The woman is married to someone else and all that happened in another lifetime."

Sam leaned forward a bit and stared David in the eye. "You've hit the nail on the head, Good Buddy. The lady *is* now married to someone else, and therein lies the problem. Lisa's husband, Raymond, is a very interesting character and plays a leading role in this drama.

I haven't exactly been sitting on my ass, you know, and twiddling my thumbs the last few days. I've been excavating way down deep past the permafrost of this Siberia. The story ain't pretty and it's just as cold. However, before I get ahead of myself, let me give you some background as a prelude to the actual plot.

Apparently, Raymond Metcalf, Lisa's significant other, was something of a boy wunderkind back in the day. He was only nineteen years old when he acquired an advanced degree from MIT in computer engineering. Initially, he worked for Microsoft, but he was a bit strange and his coworkers complained. I've never met the man, so 'a bit strange' can have a lot of different meanings. Maybe he has Asperger's Syndrome, or maybe he's some sort of pervert or belongs to a devil-worshipping cult. I couldn't pin down anything specific one way or the other. Most of his former coworkers that I located and tried to interview very delicately explained that Raymond and Microsoft just were not a good fit. Everybody chose their words very carefully because they knew he was married to a woman who worked for a lawyer, and nobody wanted to be sued for defamation of character.

Eventually, it seems that 'Raymond the Weird Wunderkind' left Microsoft and obtained a position with a global banking institution. He worked at a branch right here in Baltimore, and was responsible for overseeing the financial end of some very big investments. The client accounts represented some rather large corporations as well as very wealthy individuals. After subletting an apartment in a downtown high-rise, our gifted techie met his next-door neighbor, a legal secretary who would become his future wife. Now let's move on to the pertinent stuff like the guy's penchant for a very expensive vice and his clever modus operandi to finance his habit," Sam continued.

Chapter Twenty-Nine

"At some point during their decade of marriage, Raymond hit upon the idea that he was very adept at managing convoluted numbers and calculating odds and percentages. However, his high-level job precluded him from using his skills and insider knowledge to play the stock market. Not to be discouraged, he came up with another way to utilize his brilliant mind. He determined that he was going to indulge in some heavy-duty gambling, being snobbishly sure that the system that he had perfected in his mind could outfox the house.

However, the best-laid plans in games of chance do not always work out the way that they appear on paper or in a genius' head. Although he occasionally won money from time to time in Vegas or the casinos in the Northeast, he eventually found himself in the hole. Over time, brash and overconfident Raymond managed to gamble away the young couple's entire savings. He then tapped into IRAs, ROTHs, and even pension plans, but, eventually, all their hard-earned capital was gone. In desperation, the pair took out a second mortgage on their little house in Northeast Baltimore County.

But by now, Raymond, the poor sucker, was hooked like an addict and couldn't stop gambling. He kept tweaking his system because he just knew, in the long run, he'd be a winner and come out on top. Until then, he found that he needed to borrow money from some very unsavory and threatening loan sharks at usury rates. Unfortunately, he couldn't pay back either the principal or even the vig in a timely fashion. I was not surprised when someone told me that a few years ago reckless Raymond had a little accident during the winter. He broke his leg skiing. How strange that a catastrophe like that happened to a nerd who had never seen a ski slope in his life. I'm surmising that, by then, a desperate man was beyond scared," Sam mused.

"What to do, what to do?" the old PI intoned dramatically. "Our poor dumb schmuck suddenly found himself caught right between a rock and a hard place. Well, clever or stupid Raymond, depending on your point of view, took it to the next level. He used the bank where he was employed as his new lending institution. He started siphoning off money from client accounts that fell under his purview, and spread it out across the board, little by little, over weeks and weeks. Therefore, it wasn't noticed for almost eighteen months until the higher-ups in their lofty corner offices suddenly began to get a series of complaints at tax time about discrepancies. They immediately ordered an independent audit. It didn't take long before the jig was up for an obsequious financial analyst/accountant milquetoast.

As you can well imagine, this was quite an embarrassing situation for an international bank with a previously sterling reputation. During the mid-2000s, they had steadfastly risen above their competitors during the banking crisis when other lending institutions were coming under attack for granting subprime loans, for manipulating their numbers, and then ignominiously failing. This bank took pride in its solvency as well as its ethical and responsible financial practices. Now there was panic in the ranks thanks to one of their own trusted employees.

The executive golden boys on the board of directors and their leagues of corporate attorneys put their heads together and opted for the 'cover your ass' approach. After all, the pilfered investment accounts were federally insured and not one client would lose a penny. They did not bring charges of embezzlement against their employee because that would be admitting that they had been quite negligent in their oversight process and it would reflect badly on their august institution.

Even though Raymond had been thrown a bone, thanks to the industry gossip pipeline, he was radioactive and couldn't obtain any sort of gainful employment. Husband and wife were trying to make ends meet on Lisa's paltry little salary. Just six months ago, their modest house in the suburbs went into a foreclosure issued by the mortgage holder, and one of their cars was repossessed. All of their credit cards were maxed out with substantial debt still owed, and the interest accruing at 18%. Even the utilities were in arrears to the three-month point when the gas and electric company was about to turn off the taps."

Sam paused to gauge David's reaction. The old FBI man wanted more.

"I think there's more to this guy's Greek tragedy, Sam, so don't keep me in suspense. Even though I'm champing at the bit to connect all the dots, it's your show. It's time for your encore, my friend. Wrap it up for me all neat and tidy."

Sam gladly obliged. "During my earnest endeavors into this couple's finances, I uncovered a rather recent and puzzling anomaly. Imagine my surprise when I noticed that sudden and unexplained large installments of cash were periodically being infused into the Metcalf bank account. It was quite a coincidence that those payments showed up just a matter of days after a blackmail demand.

At first, five or ten thousand dollars went to forestall an eviction notice. Some was later drawn out in lump sums of cash that I bet went to some twitchy bookies. I personally suspect that the Metcalfs had found themselves a cash cow and were milking it for all it was worth."

David was pensive for a few moments. "So, your rationale is that Lisa Metcalf was desperate and acted on her long-ago hunch about Michael's paternity. She then told her husband her suspicions and the socially-stunted cyber genius grabbed onto a lifeline. He took a chance and sent those emails on a trip around the world before they landed on the two Abrams boys' laptops. When the devious couple were rewarded for their efforts, they knew that they were onto something big."

"That's my thinking," Sam agreed. "Initially, Lisa couldn't go directly to the Senator for hush money because, with his clout, she'd run the risk of him squashing her like a bug. She had to remain anonymous, and that's why she made Michael the fall guy in the scheme. She had no way of knowing that Michael would hear of the extortion demands and confront his father head-on while denying any participation in the fraud."

David had a question. "Do you think that Raymond Metcalf killed Jarod Abrams that night when the Senator began to have doubts that Michael was behind everything? Maybe Abrams had a second confrontation on the night of his death with Metcalf. Maybe he flatly refused to pay another cent of blackmail money and the argument got out of hand."

"Now, that's the fly in the ointment," Sam said worriedly. "Why would Raymond Metcalf even show up in person? So far, everything was being handled anonymously with the college boys as the messengers. Everything was coming up roses for the blackmailers, so why rock the boat?

In my mind, it makes absolutely no sense that Raymond would suddenly pay the Senator a visit and expose his true identity. And there's another problem with that theory. How could he have known that the person he was pretending to be was even in town, or that Michael had a face-to-face with his father that very night? Plus, the timeline for the murder is really tight. We'd have to establish two important facts.

First, we'd have to solidly prove that Raymond Metcalf was actually in Washington DC that same night, and secondly, that he had paid the Senator a visit right after Michael left the apartment. That's going to be tough. The DC police scoured every bit of camera footage and tracked down each person who entered or left the building during the crucial two-hour window of time. Raymond Metcalf was never on their radar, so, unless he was wearing Harry Potter's invisibility cloak, we're screwed!"

David frowned in concentration. "The way I see it, you *have* made some headway, Sam. That's progress. You've developed an alternate theory regarding the origin of the blackmail that the cops can trace, just like you did, after they get a proper warrant. However, there's one big stumbling block with your monumental breakthrough. We'd have to convince them to do that. I'm assuming that you found out the source of those emails by utilizing less than legal means. We just can't go to the authorities and say 'Abra Cadabra!' and produce a name out of thin air."

Sam was now also frowning because David was raining on his parade. However, the former FBI agent was still looking ahead to the next task.

"Our next hurdle is somehow placing Raymond Metcalf at the scene during the period that the coroner has established as the Senator's time of death," David mused. "Enabling Manus and Ellis to introduce another viable suspect with an agenda might throw 'reasonable doubt' into the Fed's case against Michael. That also may prevent a death sentence for him."

"Yep," Sam agreed, somewhat pacified. "That's how I read it."

"Sure, a piece of cake," David said cynically. "Somehow we need to get this Metcalf guy to admit that he and his wife were orchestrating a financial scam. How do you propose that we accomplish that, short of waterboarding the creep?"

"I guess we can ask real nicely," Sam said with a smile. That smile sent chills down David's spine.

Chapter Thirty

The Metcalf's house was a little brick Cape Cod bungalow located in the suburb of Overlea in Baltimore County. It was just like all the other homes that sat on small lots lining the quiet street. These were residences that had been built with GI loans right after young men began arriving home in mass from World War II. The servicemen were getting married in droves after the interruption in their lives. They were settling down to raise families in what, at the time, was a suburban 1950s utopia. The houses were meant to be "forever" homes, and they probably were to a generation who usually attained steady employment from the same company until they retired and were given a gold watch. However, that was a long time ago in another less complicated era.

Now the seventy-year-old residences simply looked sad and neglected, and the Metcalf one was no exception. The continuity of the roof was a choppy mosaic of different shades of shingles patching what were probably weak, leaking areas. The wrought iron railing that ran across the small front porch was blistered and rusting, and the stained cement steps were crumbling. The once proud testament to a member of "The Greatest Generation" now looked like a debilitated old senior citizen ready for the nursing home.

David and Sam had a bit of difficulty finding a parking place because none of these houses had driveways or garages. It was just after the dinner hour, so almost every available inch of parallel parking curb space had been taken up by mid-level cars and pickup trucks. Finally, they managed to squeeze

Sam's big Hummer at the end of the block perilously close to a fire hydrant.

The two men had already discussed their strategy before setting out from downtown. At their previous meeting with the legal secretary at a fast food establishment they had let her erroneously assume that David was still with the FBI. Sam had just loomed at David's side, so she probably thought that he represented the local police. They never actually claimed that they were law enforcement, but then neither had they corrected her false assumption.

The imposters hoped that would work to their advantage today with both Mr. and Mrs. Metcalf. They had timed their arrival with the expectation that the lady of the house was home from work, and her husband, who obviously didn't work, might be camped out in front of the television set after the evening meal.

With a degree of swagger, they climbed the few steps to the porch. Lisa, clad in a pair of old baggy sweats, met the two determined investigators at her front door. For a second, the surprised woman looked frightened, but then she quickly smoothed out her features to project a puzzled expression.

"Mrs. Metcalf," David said seriously, "it would seem that my associate and I have more questions for you pertaining to the Jarod Abrams murder investigation. Hopefully, this is not a bad time, but if it is, we apologize. You see, we really do need to discuss some necessary things with both you and your husband."

"My husband isn't home right now," Lisa Metcalf stuttered.

"Well, we can certainly come back to talk with him another time," Sam interjected. "However, since we are already here, we can begin to ask you our questions. I'm sure that you are eager to help us clarify some facts."

"I can't imagine how I can help," Lisa protested. "As I told you the other day, everything that I know about Jarod Abrams and Michael Wyatt happened a long time ago. It's really old news."

"Nevertheless, your cooperation in this matter would be greatly appreciated," David answered as he took a bold step forward causing Lisa to open the door even wider. When she declined to object, the two men sauntered into her small living space and gave her expectant looks.

"Sure, I suppose that I could go over things one more time for you," she said resignedly.

"Perhaps you will also be more forthcoming this evening, Mrs. Metcalf," David said ominously. "You see, my associate and I think that it's just a bit farfetched that you made a phenomenal leap of logic when you accurately 'guessed' that Abrams and Wyatt were father and son. You must have had more to go on than similar looks."

Lisa looked like a deer caught in the headlights. "I guess I'm just very observant," she mumbled.

"You must have been clairvoyant as well," Sam almost sneered. "Now, we are aware that Michael Wyatt/Devereaux left a DNA sample on a water glass in Abrams' office all those years ago. Were you responsible for sending that tumbler to a private lab for testing along with a sample from Senator Abrams?"

"I really can't remember," Lisa whispered miserably as she looked down at her hands in her lap.

"Try harder!" David insisted forcefully.

"You're badgering me and making me nervous, so I really can't think," Lisa complained.

"We're only having a nice quiet discussion right now," David clarified. "Badgering will come when you are on the witness stand and a defense attorney is the one doing the grilling. Are you truly prepared to risk perjury by lying under oath, Mrs. Metcalf?"

"What possible difference could a paternity issue make at this late date?" Lisa demanded. "This is a murder case, the police have the person responsible in custody, so isn't it all cut and dried?"

"Not quite," Sam now spoke up. "The case is all predicated on motive, and that motive was blackmail. However, I think you know that Michael Devereaux was not the one doing the blackmailing."

"Surely you're not accusing me?" Lisa asked incredulously.

"If it wasn't you, then it was your husband," David said forcefully, "and you provided him with the ammunition."

When the hostile woman simply stared at her accuser in stupefaction, David kept right on verbally punching.

"Mrs. Metcalf, we know everything about you and your husband. We know that your spouse is a tech genius who set everything in motion and thought that he had covered his ass by being cagey. However, our computer wizards are just as clever, and they traced the blackmail emails right back to this address.

We also know *your* motive. We are aware that Mr. Metcalf has a gambling problem and that you two are about to lose everything. We've looked at your financials and saw the steady influxes of cash that were deposited shortly after each blackmail payout. It seemed to be going like clockwork for months until Senator Abrams had his fill of your shenanigans. Was it at that point when your husband finally decided to grow some balls and come out of the woodwork?

We think that he made a fast trip to Washington to confront his mark face-to-face. Maybe your husband threatened to sell his knowledge to some scandal rag for a windfall if Abrams didn't agree to keep the gravy train rolling along. The Senator was a volatile man, and it isn't hard to picture the heated argument between him and your husband.

Maybe Mr. Metcalf didn't intend for the dire consequences to happen, but, nonetheless, he left a dead man behind. That's murder, Mrs. Metcalf, plain and simple! You can be arrested, as well, and be deemed an accomplice or a co-conspirator who aided and abetted a murderer. At the very least, you can be charged as an accessory after the fact."

"Raymond is not a murderer and I wasn't even there at the time!" Lisa cried out. "My husband may have a lot of faults, but he's simply not capable of doing something like that."

"Situations can certainly evolve," Sam said softly. "Moving from thwarted blackmailer to murderer isn't a stretch. Maybe Raymond didn't intend for it to happen, Lisa. I'm willing to give him the benefit of the doubt. If you weren't with him, just tell us what he told you after he got home from Washington?"

"He never went to Washington, DC," Lisa insisted. "He was actually in Atlantic City gambling on the same night that Jarod Abrams was killed."

"Maybe that's what he told you," David added. "We'll need to hear his alibi firsthand, so where is Raymond right now, Mrs. Metcalf?"

When Lisa's angry face turned stubborn, David pushed the envelope.

"Do we have to issue an all-points bulletin for your husband? Do you want him arrested and handcuffed and shoved into a squad car when he is eventually found? All kind of things can happen during arrests because adrenalin runs high in those situations and panicked people do stupid things in the heat of the moment. It would be easier if you just told us where he is so that everything can be handled quietly, and nobody gets hurt."

"He didn't do this," Lisa wailed.

"Where is he?" David insisted.

After a moment, Lisa suddenly looked defeated. "He's at Bally's in Atlantic City," she finally mumbled. "Ray likes to play Blackjack because he's perfected a system that he swears will allow him to clean up at the table."

Sam quickly strode over to a wedding photograph of the couple perched on the fireplace mantle. He adroitly snapped a picture with his phone and stepped out onto the front porch of the tiny house. He then used speed dial to make a quick call.

Chapter Thirty-One

Vincent Duffinetti answered on the first ring, and Sam got right to the heart of the matter.

"Does the Family have any reliable and discrete relatives in Atlantic City who would be willing to do a favor for their Baltimore cousins?" Sam asked.

"Is the Pope in Rome Catholic?" Duff replied sarcastically. "Of course, Sam, we have relatives all over New Jersey who work in tandem with other members of the network when it is beneficial to do so."

"Well, this may be something very beneficial for Michael," the PI stressed. "I'm sending a picture to your phone, and we need the groom in that photo found as soon as possible. His wife says that he likes to play Blackjack at Bally's on the Atlantic City Boardwalk. Hopefully, he can be located, and someone can escort him to a quiet place to find out if he visited Senator Jarod Abrams on the night of his death.

Keep the persuasion subtle, but make sure that he knows that some friends in Baltimore are sitting across from his wife right now. That may do the trick so that any rough stuff isn't necessary. If he sees the light and admits to offing the politico, we need the authorities to believe that his confession wasn't coerced by force. To wrap things up real neat and tidy, we also need him to admit that he was blackmailing Abrams and be willing to spill his guts to the cops back in Washington, DC.

"I'll set the wheels in motion," Duff promised.

When Sam returned to the Metcalf living room, Lisa was weeping softly. David looked to Sam with raised eyebrows and the PI fielded the tacit question with a quick wink.

145

Sam again sat down on the sofa next to David and assumed an authoritative demeanor.

"Mrs. Metcalf, I've made arrangements for someone to find your husband in Atlantic City. They'll talk with him at length and get back to me. Right now, you have to make a statement outlining the whole scenario, and then we'll eventually see if your husband's version matches yours."

That prompted David to pull out his cellphone and start making adjustments before carefully laying it on the coffee table between himself and the distraught secretary.

"I'm going to be recording everything that you say, Lisa, just so there are no misunderstandings or discrepancies later on in the process. I want you to start at the very beginning fifteen years ago when you worked for Abrams and first met the man whom you knew as Michael Wyatt at the time. Be precise and thorough and don't leave anything out. Take the saga right up to the time of the Senator's murder. Are you willing to do that? I think that it will be less stressful for you to talk about it right here in your own home rather than at the police station."

Lisa nodded miserably, blew her nose, and took a deep breath. She indicated that she was ready to go forward with a jerky nod of her head.

David suddenly was all business. He was now in his comfort zone because he had done this drill countless times before when he had been an agent with the FBI. He knew that he had to dot every "i" and cross every "t" so that it was airtight.

Pushing the record function button on the phone started the process. David began the narrative by identifying himself, and then giving the date, time, and location of a forthcoming conversation between himself and Lisa Metcalf. He then made Lisa identify herself and state that what she was about to say was admitted freely, and she was under no duress to provide

146

the following facts as she knew them. Then, very hesitantly, the story started to spool out.

"Fifteen years ago I worked as a legal secretary for Jarod Abrams. Back then, he wasn't a senator yet. He had been a state district attorney but later he stepped down from that position to practice private law out of an office on Baltimore's Inner Harbor. I think that he was simply killing time while waiting for a judgeship to be offered.

Anyway, one day Michael Wyatt stopped by unexpectedly. Back then, that's the name that he was using instead of Devereaux. I recognized him, of course, because everybody in the city knew of him. He was something of a hometown celebrity because he had just finished the construction of magnificent Symington Place, an over-the-top glamorous project of downtown condominiums. He was also young and very handsome, so you certainly remembered his face.

Mr. Wyatt hadn't made an appointment to see Mr. Abrams, and I was surprised when my boss agreed to meet with him. They had a short, quiet session behind closed doors, and I only interrupted once when Mr. Abrams asked me to bring a bottle of water and a glass for Mr. Wyatt. Soon after, Mr. Wyatt left.

Of course, I was just a lowly secretary, so I wasn't privy to what went on during their meeting. However, I thought it was strange when my boss gave me a package to take to a medical lab the very next day. I was surprised by that request because Mr. Abrams usually only concerned himself with corporate law, like mergers and acquisitions, at that point in time.

Well, I'm certainly not proud of what I did next, but I was curious. I opened the package and found one of our office tumblers in a plastic bag. There was also a little Ziploc bag inside with some tufts of dark hair that had obviously been pulled out by the roots. You could see little tags of tissue at

147

the ends. Each bag was labeled—one with an 'A' and the other with a 'B.'

Well, I'm certainly not a complete idiot. It was obvious that Mr. Abrams wanted to compare some DNA samples, and it didn't take a rocket scientist to make an educated guess of who was being compared to whom. One week later, a letter arrived marked 'Personal and Confidential' from the medical lab. As I said, I'm not proud of my actions, but it didn't stop me from steaming open the letter. It confirmed my suspicions. There was a definite familial match on the paternal side of the spectrum.

Therefore, it came as no surprise when Mr. Abrams began assembling briefs and motions to represent Mr. Wyatt in an upcoming Federal trial. From their interactions in the office, it was quite evident that there was no love lost between father and son. Their relationship was predicated on the business at hand, and it was only a temporary liaison brought about by necessity. After Mr. Wyatt was acquitted of all charges, he abruptly left town. To my knowledge, he and Mr. Abrams never met again.

You really must understand, that I never dreamed of doing anything with the knowledge that I had discovered. I'm not a sociopath by any means. However, Jarod Abrams was as close to one as you could get because he lacked a conscience. He wanted what he wanted, and nobody had better get in his way. When the federal judgeship was awarded to someone else, he rallied after that disappointment and decided to run for a state Senate seat in Congress.

Of course, he was victorious, and he managed to keep on winning every time an election rolled around. He quickly made the upscale move to DC and left me behind without a second thought. Life was all about him and what *he* wanted. We had been in an intimate relationship for some time, but he threw me to the curb without a backward glance. Apparently, I was just a handy and more than willing convenience all those years. Now he was moving on to greener pastures.

I was hurt beyond reason, but I wasn't vengeful. I didn't go to his wife and rat him out. I moved on with my own life and tried to put everything behind me like a cautionary tale. Eventually, I met Raymond Metcalf, a gentle and kind man who seemed to genuinely love me. It was like a breath of fresh air to be seen in public hanging onto his arm. There would be no sneaking around with Ray. He was beyond smart in so many ways. He was a technological genius who had an important job with a worldwide bank. He moved to Baltimore to work at one of its branches here in the city. I was so proud to become his wife.

The beginning years of our marriage were wonderful, but Ray always had visions of something greater out there on the horizon You see, his brilliant mind doesn't work like yours or mine. He thinks in a three dimensional realm when figuring out a logistical problem. For him, it's all about swirling numbers in his head and their possible applications. He's always doodling different equations on scraps of paper. He even dreams about numbers. Sometimes, I'd wake up in the middle of the night and find him sitting at the kitchen table working out a complicated math sequence. One day, he told me that he had made a breakthrough. He had devised a system that would beat the odds at any game of chance.

At first, it was fun to take day trips to Atlantic City or weekend junkets to Las Vegas so that Ray could test his hypothesis. He'd gamble for a while and then we'd have dinner and see a show. Sometimes, Ray won, but most times his contrived 'system' failed and he lost. However, he never gave up and just went back to the proverbial drawing board to find the error in his thinking. It was an insidious thing, and

I should have seen it much earlier. Eventually, I realized that my husband had developed an addiction to gambling and he just couldn't stop.

Over the next two years, we got deeper and deeper into debt. We refinanced the house, I sold my engagement ring, and we maxed out our credit cards. We did everything that we could to stay afloat and keep the wolf from the door. All the while, Ray kept promising me that success was just around the corner. When the loan sharks got involved, it frightened me beyond reason. When they broke one of Ray's legs with a baseball bat, he knew that he had to do something drastic. That was when he began siphoning funds from client accounts at the bank. Of course, there came a day of reckoning and he was fired. He was lucky that he didn't have to do any jail time.

After that disaster, Ray couldn't find work. Even the 7-11 wouldn't hire him because the bank blackballed him every time a new prospective employer checked his references. My salary was small and wasn't even enough to pay the utilities and groceries much less a hefty mortgage payment. We were about to be evicted when I came up with a last resort option."

David threw Sam a sidelong glance. Now they were getting to the heart of the matter. Hopefully, it would be enough to set Michael free.

Chapter Thirty-Two

"Please," Lisa begged, "you have to understand how desperate we were at the time. Ray and I were one step away from living on the street like bag people. At night when I couldn't sleep, I'd go back over the decisions that I had made in my life that had brought me to this terrible point. I realized that I could have had a different future, but I had wasted years on a man who was never destined to love me. It was like picking at a hangnail. I couldn't let it alone, and I just started nursing the hurt surrounding my past with a narcissist.

Jarod Abrams had it all—money, power, a tolerant wife, two intelligent sons, and a lock on a Senate seat that he would probably hold until he was old and senile. It just wasn't fair that he could use and abuse people whenever he chose and then go on his merry way without a pang of guilt. He needed to feel threatened and afraid just like I was feeling. For once in his life, that man needed to know how it feels not to be in control."

Lisa sighed deeply and looked to her two inquisitors with a pleading expression.

"Do you get it?" she asked pitifully.

"I think that we can understand your motivation," David agreed, "but you have to spell it out for the record, Mrs. Metcalf. Explain everything that you and your husband did next."

Another sigh from Lisa heralded the rest of the story.

"I told my husband about the familial connection between Jarod and Michael Wyatt. I didn't specify how I had come into that knowledge, nor did I tell Ray of my protracted affair with the Senator when he was a lawyer in private practice.

'That guy's not squeaky clean,' I told my husband. 'He has skeletons in his closet. There's a very damning one that he's prevented from seeing the light of day for almost two decades. We can threaten to open that Pandora's Box to expose him for the callous jerk that he has always been. His only recourse will be to pay us to keep silent so that his image remains intact.'

Ray wasn't on board, at first. He claimed that I was playing with fire and it could be dangerous for me.

'The man might be a cad, Lisa, but he's also a lawyer and knows all the legal tricks to shut you down,' Ray had worried. 'He could sue us for slander, defamation of character, and probably a bunch of other things.'

'Let him sue us, Hon, I had told my husband. We don't have any money for him to collect. I just want to make him sweat for once.'"

Lisa's face softened suddenly as she pictured her husband's part in the plot.

"When I just kept perseverating on revenge against Jarod, Ray came up with his own suggestion. He didn't want me confronting someone head on who could be dangerous. He thought it prudent to stick to the shadows and work through an intermediary, or intermediaries, in this case. We chose the two sons to be the messengers, and we made Michael Wyatt the logical bad guy.

I guess that I should regret using Jarod's sons in that way, but it seemed the safest option to keep Ray and I one-step removed. Those kids were winding up years in an Ivy League college where they had gotten an education that cost a mint. Jarod had probably paid enough tuition money through the years to cover the cost of our house as well as all our other debts. The Abrams family had it all and we had nothing. I needed to balance the scales a bit.

Ray is a tech genius, and he easily rerouted our emails around the world until they landed on Jason and Justin's laptop. We worded every sentence very carefully. We never threatened the boys. We just made them aware of the facts and hinted that their father might be amenable to a monetary solution to keep the damning information from becoming an embarrassment to them and also their mother. Of course, we signed the emails with just the name 'Michael.' I had no idea where the real Michael had gone. It had been years since anyone reported seeing him. For all I knew, he could have moved out of the country, or he could have even died.

Well, our plan worked like a charm. We'd name a figure and demanded that it be paid with a cashier's check sent to a post office box on the Eastern Shore of Maryland. Ray has a cousin living in Salisbury who retrieved the letters and then mailed them to us. At first, our demand was small—just $5,000 to test the waters. When it quickly arrived, we gave the money to our bankruptcy lawyer, and he was able to stave off the sheriff posting an eviction notice on our door. Other $5,000 dribs and drabs went towards utilities and car payments.

We were slowly climbing out of a very deep hole, but it was like digging out of the abyss with a teaspoon. We needed a quicker fix, so we raised our payoff figure. At first, it was $20,000 a pop, but our last demand was for $50,000. We said in our email that this amount would be the last installment on what was owed for a life lived in ignominy.

Well, we waited and waited, but that last cashier's check never arrived. We had gone to the well many times over the months, but now the water seemed to have dried up. We still had troublesome remaining debt. It wasn't even close to being

153

over for us, so Ray did the only thing that he knew how to do. He went back to gambling," Lisa finally concluded the tale.

"Now tell us about the sequel, Lisa," David prodded. "I'm sure that you and your husband didn't just quietly fold your tents and slink away into the desert. You had too much at stake to give up that easily. Who actually went to Washington to see Abrams? Was it you or your husband? Perhaps you both went to confront him. You threatened exposure, maybe claimed that you were going to the media with your story. Abrams' house of cards would come tumbling down if he didn't comply and pay you off one last time.

We've heard that the Senator was a snake, so maybe he threatened you right back with bodily harm. In a panicked state, either you or your husband tried to defend yourselves. The Scotch bottle was right there, and it suddenly became a weapon to fend him off."

"No, no, no," Lisa Metcalf wailed. "Neither of us went to Washington. We heard about the murder on the news just like everyone else. You can check with my job. I was at the office the day of the incident and I didn't set a toe out the door once I got home. We only have one car, and Ray had taken that to the casino in Atlantic City where he spent the night at the Blackjack table."

When David couldn't shake the woman's adamant claim of innocence, he pushed the end button on the phone recording.

"Your alibi will certainly be thoroughly documented," he stated firmly. "Now, we'll just have to settle back to await what your husband has to say when he is confronted in New Jersey. That could take a while, so why don't you play the gracious hostess and make a pot of coffee. However, before you disappear into the kitchen, please hand over your own cell phone!"

Lisa Metcalf certainly wasn't very happy, but she sullenly complied. Sam flicked on the small flat screen television and the odd trio watched tedious sitcoms until the 11 o'clock news came on. That was followed by the various late night talk show clowns. At just after midnight, Sam's phone vibrated in his pocket. It was Duff with an up-to-the-minute report. Sam walked back out onto the porch to continue the conversation.

"I've got some good news and some bad news," the old Italian said. "Which do you want to hear first?"

Chapter Thirty-Three

"Just lay it all out, chapter and verse," Sam encouraged.

"Well, our handy associates in Atlantic City found the dude exactly where you thought he would be," Duff explained. "Those gentlemen very cordially extended an invitation for Metcalf to join them in one in the hotel's suites. Apparently, this flake had some past experience with enforcers, and he was falling all over himself to be cooperative. Crank that up a few notches when he was made aware that someone back in Baltimore was babysitting his wife. He readily copped to the blackmail scheme, but vehemently denied visiting Abrams in Washington or having anything to do with his murder. Claimed that he was at the same Blackjack table on the night in question.

Apparently, one of the inquisitors has a second cousin who is a pit boss at Bally's. That particular relative checked the logbook as well as past footage from the 'eye in the sky.' Unfortunately, it corroborates the guy's story. The doofus was sitting on a stool at the table losing to the tune of over forty thou before he went bust and they cut off his line of credit."

Sam groaned in frustration. "It's certainly not everything that we had hoped for, but at least it's something to take to Michael's attorneys," he said morosely. "It will work to take motive off the table. Unfortunately, it's just a tiny baby step chipping away at all the other circumstantial crap, and Michael's far from out of the woods, yet."

"I hear you," Duff agreed. "For what it's worth, a New Jersey contingent is personally escorting Metcalf back to his front door in Baltimore. They should be arriving around 3 am.

You can then do whatever it is that you need to do on your end. Sorry that we couldn't be more help."

"Thanks, Buddy," Sam said gratefully, "I know I owe you big time."

"Good friends don't keep a running tab, Sam," Duff said softly. "Let me know if there is anything else you need."

David knew from Sam's expression when he returned to the living room that their plan had not gone as expected. He waited for the PI's next gambit.

"Your husband is on his way home to you," Sam said softly. "Luckily, his story matches yours. However, please do not feel complacent. You two are in a big world of trouble for the blackmail and extortion that you systematically perpetrated. Make no mistake, you will be prosecuted for your criminal actions, and we are certainly not done with you by a long shot. My partner and I will be on you like white on rice if you try to renege in any way.

The first step that we will take tonight is to file a copy of this recorded dialogue with the local branch of the FBI who will then forward a copy to the Federal Prosecutor in DC. Michael Devereaux's lawyers will also get their own copy.

My advice to you and your husband is to try and get ahead of this runaway train. Present yourself to the authorities first thing in the morning and confess your sins. The Feds will already have a copy of your forthright statement that was obtained tonight. It's a better option than having squad cars pull up in your little neighborhood, break down your door, and drag you and your husband away in handcuffs. If I were you, I'd opt for a dignified exit plan."

"We'll be there," Lisa mumbled while staring down at her hands again.

"Don't be foolish. See that you are," Sam threatened. "You certainly wouldn't want us coming after you!"

"Damn, I thought we were going to hit a homerun tonight," David complained as they returned to his apartment to make flash drive copies of the recorded confession.

"Yeah, I know," Sam agreed, "we didn't manage to hit it out of the ballpark tonight."

"That's true," David mused, "but it still was a lifesaver in a way. At least it took motive off the table for Michael as well as negating that this was a premeditated act. The enormity of that could have meant a death sentence for him if he were found guilty."

"There are too many 'ifs' in this situation for my liking," Sam decreed. "I like my mysteries solved with no dangling loose ends. If Metcalf didn't kill Abrams and neither did Michael, then who did the dirty deed?"

"The man had a lot of enemies, so that's like looking for one little guppy in an ocean of fish," David decreed. "Michael's trial is happening in less than a month, so there's no time for a new scavenger hunt to find little Nemo at this late date. We can keep plugging away at things, but I doubt we're going to find a solution to the problem in time."

"I don't usually agree with you, Mr. Former G-Man, but, unfortunately, this time I think you're right. We've exhausted the usual viable options."

David looked askance at Sam. This rare capitulation was out of character for the retired CIA operative who usually never accepted defeat. Suddenly, David was uncomfortable, but he didn't want to explore Sam's psyche just yet. David thought that maybe he was just overly worn out and simply jumping to a wrong conclusion about the man. However, he'd keep a close eye on the investigator to see if he was up to something shifty on the illegal side of the equation.

By this time, the two men had already dropped off a copy of Lisa Metcalf's damning statement at the FBI Bureau office in Woodlawn. Now, they were parking in front of Ellis Faraday's house in suburban Worthington Valley. Although the sun was barely coming up, they, nonetheless, pounded on his front door until the sleepy and rumpled lawyer was finally looking up at them and responding with a growl.

"This better be good, guys!"

"It is," they agreed in unison.

~~~~~~~~~~

Later that afternoon, Attiq Kabli and Jesse Cormier were also banging on another door that belonged to the Federal Prosecutor in Washington DC. The two Metro detectives were not happy.

"The old office grapevine says that you're contemplating offering this Devereaux dude a manslaughter plea," Jesse said antagonistically. "Man, that arrest was a righteous bust. Attiq and I had all the bases covered and nailed down tight. So, please tell us lowly peons why you're throwing in the towel without even a fight? Man, that just doesn't compute!" the man ended his tirade with his trademark euphemism.

The Federal Prosecutor sighed as he stared at their outraged faces.

"I'm simply being pragmatic, gentleman. The confession by Abrams' former secretary and her husband admitting that they were behind the blackmail puts a serious crimp in our case. Everything that we now have in the way of evidence is circumstantial, and we have no motive except for calling it a crime of passion.

Devereaux has already admitted that he visited his old man that night, but denies that he killed him. He claims that he left him fuming, but living and breathing. So, there's reasonable doubt. On the flip side, if we continue to go after first degree murder, his attorneys could suddenly change his 'not guilty' plea midstream during the trial if it looks like the jury isn't buying Devereaux's version of things. Ellis Faraday and Manus Kirshner are shrewd litigators, and they could amend the plea to 'acting under extreme emotional distress' or even self-defense. Devereaux could suddenly claim that Abrams came at him with a knife or was trying to choke him. We know there was evidence of a struggle in that kitchen.

So, it's a crap shoot, gentleman, pure and simple. Make no mistake, I don't like to lose, but that just may happen if I'm not proactive now. If Devereaux takes a manslaughter deal, he'll still get substantial jail time. I'll make sure of it."

"Anybody with a brain in their head will convict on murder one with the evidence that we got for you," Attiq argued.

"You would think so," the lawyer agreed. "However, juries can be fickle and swayed by who and what they see and hear. Michael Devereaux is a very handsome man, so most likely any young women on the panel will unconsciously fall in love with that innocent-looking persona, and they would never allow themselves to imagine him committing murder.

Any older women on the jury will hear his sad story about being abandoned and neglected as a child and they'll want to mother him. Male jurors will see him as a personification of the American Dream—a kid from the streets who made good on his own in spite of his deprived beginnings.

Just picture the courtroom, Detectives. Michael Devereaux's attorneys will make sure to have his adoring and supportive wife sitting right behind him along with a row of four little apple-cheeked Kewpie dolls that make up his family. The twelve people sitting in the jury box will see a man who got on with his life a long time ago and didn't look back. They'll see a loving, kind husband and father who never denied his children. In the meantime, they'll paint Abrams as a callous, unfeeling ogre in the fairy tale."

"Couldn't you soften their perception of the Senator by bringing up the fact that, once upon a time, he actually went to bat for his son and defended him against a bunch of federal charges," Attiq asked. "That may indicate that he had some regrets and was trying to make amends for being an asshole."

"That's a double-edged sword," the prosecutor responded. "Faraday and Kirshner could rebut that by saying that the Senator did that out of self-interest rather than paternal fealty. He didn't want his callousness to be exposed. That would also open the door to the fact that Devereaux was Abrams' target when he was Maryland's State Attorney. They'll say that he had a vicious vendetta against a kid barely in his twenties. They'll allege that the only reason he later had a temporary aberration in his force field was because he had come to realize he was in a very precarious position. If Devereaux went down, then so did he along with all of his grand plans for a political future."

"Sometimes, this job sucks," Jesse informed the man in front of him. "We bust our asses to get the goods, and you people in the justice business twist and reshape things so that the real truth is hardly recognizable anymore. You're all a slick pack of jackals worried about your careers. So, in my opinion, the lot of you are just as bad as the warped politicos on Capitol Hill."

Chapter Thirty-Four

Later that day, Ellis and Manus were patiently laying out the exact same scenarios to Michael.

"We can certainly reject the offer of manslaughter and move forward with a jury trial for murder one, Michael. However, we'd be rolling the dice. Do you really want to gamble with your life?"

Michael looked stubborn, so Manus spoke up. "If you took the manslaughter deal, there would be no whimsical jury to worry about who would be deciding your future. Of course, you'd have to throw yourself on the mercy of the court and allocute in front of a judge about your alleged actions that night. However, before the presiding judge passes sentence, we could parade dozens of character witnesses before him who can attest to your impeccable sterling character before this unfortunate event. We could even argue that Abrams forced your hand by threatening the people that you care about in your life."

"I'm not going to confess to a crime that I didn't commit," Michael stated unequivocally. "How can my children ever look their father in the eye again when they think that I killed my own? I just won't do it!"

"They won't stop loving you, my boy," Manus said softly. "Nothing that you could say would ever negate that feeling."

Michael shook his head. "Look, Manus, even if I did plead guilty to manslaughter, I'd probably go to jail for a very long time in a prison that is over 3,000 miles away from them. I'll start fading away as any kind of father, or even a husband, for that matter. I'd rather tell the truth and take my chances!"

"Please think on it a bit," Ellis prompted. "The offer will probably remain on the table right up until your trial in a few weeks."

Before the two men left, Michael made an unusual request. He asked to speak with Manus alone about something of a personal nature. Ellis looked intrigued, but professionalism prevented him from asking the nature of the proposed discussion. When it was just Manus and Michael sitting across from one another, the accused man got right to the point.

"Listen, my friend, if this all goes down the tubes and I crash and burn, please make sure that Amy and the children are taken care of financially. You know of all my offshore accounts, so parcel it out under the table as necessary. I don't want that part of their life to change even though I'm no longer there to provide for their futures."

The old lawyer nodded. "Of course, Michael. I can be pretty wily when I put my mind to it. I'll set up trust funds and create other tax-free vehicles right under the noses of the IRS. Those bean counters will never suspect a thing. Amy can stay in the house in San Francisco for as long as she likes, and the children can go to the schools of their choosing when the time comes for advanced education. However, it's possible that you may be taking care of business yourself. Keep the faith, Laddie. Things may look pretty bleak right now, but it ain't over till it's over."

~~~~~~~~~

It took Michael a few sleepless nights to get in the right frame of mind for his next discussion. He had to separate himself from his emotions. Just as he had done when he was a child being raped, he had to find that space in his head where he could escape the harsh reality of his situation. It was a totally numb sort of place where he felt nothing. Now, it was going to be the single most difficult thing for him to do when his wife visited via a television screen.

Amy looked lost and strained when Michael first saw her face flash up on the small viewer. He steeled himself for the additional hurt that he was going to inflict on his sweet wife.

"Amy," he began forcefully, "this has to be the last time that you visit. You need to go home to the children. You've been commuting back and forth across the continent for months, and it has to stop now."

"But I want to be here and a supportive presence during your upcoming trial," Amy insisted.

"But I don't want you here!" Michael answered. "When it's all over, Manus will telephone to tell you the verdict. If I'm convicted, then it falls to you to somehow explain that to the children in a way that they can understand. I also don't want you or the kids or your family anywhere on the East Coast when my sentence is handed down. It will be a media circus at that point, and I don't want my loved ones' faces splashed across the Internet on YouTube videos."

"Michael," Amy said with tears in her eyes, "you may be acquitted."

"I think that's an unlikely outcome," Michael insisted, "and you need to realize that fact up front. Amy, you're living in a fantasy world. Life is harsh, unfeeling, and sometimes unfair. Believe me, I know that firsthand. For some of us, there are no happy endings. I tried to warn you a long time ago. We should never have married because I had a toxic past that finally managed to catch up with me. Now, beside ruining your life, I've screwed up four others. I am so very sorry."

Amy was now openly weeping, and even though it broke Michael's heart, he still had more to say.

"For once in your life, Amy, face reality and be reasonable. If you truly love me, then you'll do as I'm asking. Cut your losses and run. After all the notoriety calms down, file for a quiet divorce and get on with your life. You deserve someone so much more worthy than me, and, hopefully, one day you'll find him."

"I don't want to get on with a life without you in it," she hiccupped.

"Well, then you're being selfish because you're not thinking of the children and what's best for them. Kids need stability and a mother and a father to guide them through life and keep them safe. I'm trusting you to make it right for them. Move on and hold your head up. None of this was your fault. I allowed my family to become collateral damage in my war, and I'll never forgive myself for that. Now, please leave and don't come back again!"

Michael abruptly stood and motioned to the guard that he was ready to return to his cell. It took every ounce of his strength not to look back to view the traumatic carnage that he had left in his wake.

Amy all but ran from the building. Sam was standing on the sidewalk awaiting her return. He had an inkling of what Michael might do, so he had come to Washington to drive Amy to her visit with her husband. The PI held the quivering and sobbing woman to his chest and waited out the storm. Right about now, Michael Devereaux was not Sam's most favorite person, but the wise PI had known that this wasn't a surprising sacrifice on Michael's part. He was valiantly trying to prepare Amy for the worst in private rather than in an open courtroom.

"He's given up, Sam," Amy wailed. "He's given up on me and the children."

"No, Sweetheart," Sam sought to comfort her, "the only person that he's given up on is himself."

Chapter Thirty-Five

Time marched on, and soon it was the week before the trial. Although Michael's daily routine hadn't varied, he was now living in that walled-off place in his mind for most of the long hours spent in his cell. His bunkmate wisely kept his distance and they barely exchanged any words. Then, just three days before opening arguments were to take place in a courtroom, Michael was abruptly transferred into another cell somewhere deeper in the labyrinth from hell.

Another prisoner was already there, and this new bunkmate was intimidatingly huge. He gave Michael a mocking, cruel smirk that made the hairs on the back of the younger man's neck prickle. The giant was an unfamiliar face, a new addition delivered by the prison bus just that afternoon. The tattooed, tough guy looked Michael up and down with a dispassionate air as if he was nothing more than a side of beef hanging in a butcher shop.

Michael sensed this ominous, creepy perusal didn't bode well for his own continued good health, and he was right. That very first night, after the overhead lights were extinguished, the new convict proceeded to reach up and haul Michael from his bunk by the thin undershirt that he wore. With a menacing thrust of his bulked up body, the ogre then pushed the ambushed man up against the concrete wall and leered into his face.

"I need to get up real close in your personal space so that I can deliver a message, pretty boy," he hissed.

Although Michael was terrified because he guessed the man's depraved and dangerous intent, that did not stop him from instinctively bringing a knee upward into the looming man's groin and slithering out of his startled grasp. With a bravado he didn't really feel, Michael confronted the now doubled-over angry prisoner.

"If you think that you can fuck me, well *fuck you*, because the only way that's going to happen is if you kill me first!"

"So, the little tiger has teeth," the large man taunted softly. "Let's see what you're really made of, candy ass!"

It didn't take but a few minutes before he had a thick arm around Michael's neck, applying more and more pressure until sudden shooting flashes of bright light danced before the trapped man's eyes. He couldn't draw a breath as the blood flow delivering needed oxygen to his brain and lungs was cut off. Michael's last thought before he lost consciousness was that it wasn't taking him long to die.

~~~~~~~~~

But Michael did not die that night. He awoke, mentally confused, in what he recognized as the prison infirmary. It was familiar to him because he had been medically examined here by a doctor when he had first been incarcerated. He was now stretched out on a narrow cot and, of course, one wrist and one ankle were handcuffed to the bed frame. However, there were no IV lines or wires connected to his body. At least that was a positive note, but then Michael began to remember, and his heart stuttered in his chest. He took a quick inventory of his body. If he had been raped, wouldn't he be aware of pain from brutally stretched and torn tissue? Try as he might, he couldn't discern any discomfort anywhere. So, why was he here? What had been done to him while he was unconscious?

Seeing that his latest patient was now awake, the prison physician made his way over to the bed. Apparently, Michael was the ward's only occupant right now, so the doctor took a few minutes to apprise him of his condition.

"You were transferred in from your cell after 'lights out' last night, Mr. Devereaux. You were unconscious at that time, but your cellmate stated that he witnessed you having a seizure. He was responsible for alerting the guards of the situation."

"That's not what I remember," Michael stated emphatically.

The doctor looked at his patient for a brief second, and then explained that it was actually very normal not to remember a seizure, and to be confused after awakening from one.

"So," Michael asked hesitantly, "were there any signs of physical trauma when I was brought in?"

"None at all," the physician reassured him. "Your fellow cellmate said he made sure that you didn't hurt yourself while you were flailing. You really should thank him for his quick thinking when you are returned to your quarters. Things could have been a lot worse.

Now that you're awake, we've scheduled a few tests at the local hospital. We'll need to rule out the presence of a brain tumor. Most likely, if everything is negative on the MRI, you'll be back here later this evening and I'll clear you medically so that you can be sent back to the unit for the night."

Chapter Thirty-Six

As the doctor had promised, Michael was approached by two prison guards that same afternoon. They released his shackles, threw a clean set of orange scrubs on the bed, and told him to get dressed while under their watchful eyes. Afterwards, a chain went around his waist and his manacled hands were secured to the center steel ring. Shackles connected by another length of chain were secured to his ankles. There wasn't much leeway in the ankle links. When Michael began walking out of the infirmary sandwiched between the two guards, he had to shuffle along slowly as best as he could to keep pace with them.

Nothing was said as the three men slowly moved along the corridors until they came to a steel door. One of the guards swiped his badge across its metal plate, and the red button immediately turned to green. When the other guard shoved on the access bar, fresh air flooded in and Michael felt the sun on his face for the first time in months. The welcome warmth didn't last very long because he was quickly hustled into the back of a prison transportation van.

One of his captors climbed into the driver's seat that was protected from any possible physical threat by a grid of steel mesh separating him from the cargo area. Michael was shoved through the back doors onto a hard metal bench that ran the length of the rear compartment. He slid back against the wall and stared at the remaining sentry, who claimed his own seat opposite his prisoner.

His keeper was grim-faced and armed to the teeth with the latest defensive gadgets. There was a Taser hooked on his belt right next to a pair of handcuffs, a baton, and a holstered pistol. Some sort of communicator hung from a belt loop, and a short-barreled riot gun was nestled on his lap. He looked to be about Michael's age, and when he gave his prisoner a cursory glance, Michael saw that his eyes were blue and hard.

When everything was secured to the guard's satisfaction, he reached an arm up and rapped on the metal ceiling.

"Let's roll and get this tin can on the road," he yelled to his partner.

The big V8 engine roared to life and they were suddenly on the move. Michael had to brace his feet on the floor to keep from sliding from side to side as the van negotiated turn after turn until the pace finally leveled out. It was at that point when Michael's guard did a strange thing. He carefully laid his shotgun on the floor, took out a set of keys on a ring, and reached over to release Michael's hands from his restraints. Then he tossed the ring into Michael's lap and told him to take care of business with the ankle chains.

Michael was stunned, and for just a second wondered if this was a setup. If Michael complied, was this guard then going to pick up that shotgun and blast him into little pieces, claiming afterwards that the prisoner was an imminent threat during an escape attempt?

"C'mon, get a move on, buddy," the suddenly impatient guard urged. "We've got just a small window of time to make this happen."

Michael was dumbfounded as he noticed the guard begin to quickly strip off his own uniform. Now Michael's own blue eyes turned hard and ominous. When the other man looked up, he snickered.

"Don't sweat it, Devereaux. You aren't on my dance card—not even close. No nooners for you. So, start getting out of those prisoner scrubs 'cause we need to swap identities. When we get to the admitting bay at the hospital ER, you're going to be me."

The guard had removed his brown kepi cap and Michael saw an abundance of thick dark hair. Without his uniform, Michael realized that the two men were both of similar height and weight. Maybe it wasn't a stretch for them to pull this off. Perhaps the hospital personnel might be too preoccupied to realize that they weren't actually ministering to the same man whose face had been splashed across the news several months ago.

Michael was about to question the "who" and the "why" when the guard continued his instructions.

"When we get to the hospital, just act like you're some swaggering Gestapo storm trooper. Get me admitted, and then, while I'm getting my poor brain buzzed, get into the passenger seat of the van. My partner will drive you two blocks south. There will be a black Chevy sedan idling at the curb. Then the new guy at the wheel of that car will take over and whisk you away from all this high drama."

"You really think this will go off without a hitch?" Michael asked skeptically.

"Well, it's been working so far," the guard assured him. "Oh, before I forget—Tony says, 'Good Luck,' and he hopes there's no hard feelings about the choke hold. He had to make things look authentic."

When Michael threw the guard a puzzled look, the man went on to explain.

"Tony is that over-muscled, ugly monster who made sure to get you to the infirmary. He was forced to use the only skills that he had to get the job done so that we could take over and do our thing. He's not the brightest bulb in the box, but he follows orders. Most times, he's a real convenient tool to have in our workshop."

Michael stayed silent, but he suspected that he knew who was really behind this audacious and daring caper. He wisely decided not to put his current ally on the spot by asking. Even if this escape didn't pan out, somehow it comforted Michael to know that his good friends were trying to do the impossible to rescue him.

An hour later, the "impossible" became not only possible, but also a reality. Michael was already in another state on his way freedom.

Chapter Thirty-Seven

That same evening, Michael's daredevil escape was all over the nightly news. The sheer panache of the act served to catapult the Houdini-like escapee to the top of the FBI's Most Wanted list. All-points bulletins were issued in states up and down the East Coast as well as the Midwest and the Great Lakes area. The San Francisco FBI had the Devereaux mansion on Steiner Street staked out around the clock. On a less publicized note, two prison guard imposters were also being sought in connection with the spontaneous disappearance, but they appeared to be in the wind as well.

"That Devereaux guy has some serious juju and real freaky connections," Jesse Cormier said with a wise nod of his head. "Now, why doesn't that surprise me in this fakakta town?" he added cynically.

The DC detective and his partner were now back at their downtown headquarters watching a television screen that had been put on mute. Attiq looked at his counterpart with his own question evident in his puzzled expression

"Okay, Jess, I understand the 'juju' part, but what's with 'fakakta?' Is that even a word?"

"It most assuredly is," Jesse replied smugly. "It's a Yiddish word that means something is all a bunch of crap. My wife tells me that about my brilliant ideas all the time. Well, maybe I'm still thinking fakakta thoughts, but now I'm looking at them from a new perspective."

"Oh, please share your fakakta insights, Partner," Attiq said with a smile. "I know how your mind works, so maybe I'll understand your thought process even if your wife doesn't."

Jesse sat down at his desk across from Attiq and put his feet up.

"Devereaux seems like he's a really intelligent dude," the detective began. "So, now I'm wondering why someone who is so smart left a breadcrumb trail a mile wide after Abrams' murder. Why did he make it so easy for us to find him?"

"I've got another Yiddish word for you, Partner—*chutzpah*," Attiq teased.

Jesse ignored the remark and continued with his theory. "Devereaux hadn't seen his father in years. They were over and done a long time ago. He chose to move as far away from his old man as possible on the complete other coast of the United States. Against all odds, that disavowed, illegitimate son somehow manages to make good on his own. He becomes successful, marries, sets down new roots, has a family, and everything is copacetic.

We now know that he definitely wasn't into blackmail. Hell, the guy's a millionaire so why try to bleed a midlevel politico for what was probably bupkis to someone like Devereaux? Apparently, he had only come to Washington from San Francisco to confront his father about the threats that the asshole Senator was making against some of his old friends. If Devereaux had returned to administer long overdue payback, wouldn't he have been more careful and stealthier? The man actually left his fingerprints on the murder weapon, for God's sake. I'm not buying it. He's not that dumb or careless."

"Maybe he panicked," Attiq theorized. "That can happen to the most intellectually brilliant person."

Jesse didn't agree. "Did the guy look like someone who would panic when we first interrogated him? When he didn't immediately clam up when his lawyers made an appearance, I thought we had everything going for us, and we could crack him wide open. Surprisingly, it seemed just the opposite. He

175

appeared to be waiting for us to make the giant leaps of logic and to figure it all out properly. Maybe he really was telling the truth all along."

"I don't know about that. What you can't refute, Jesse, is the fact that eventually he ran. An innocent man doesn't run," Attiq insisted.

Jesse considered that statement before responding. "Maybe that's because he had finally given up on the system—on us. We felt complacent because we were certain that we had the guilty perp, and we stopped considering anyone else. His trial was just days away and he was looking at a slam-dunk conviction. Here's another new word for you, Partner— '*pis aller.*' It's of French origin and it means 'last resort.' Escaping prison was a last desperate act on Devereaux's part because he was out of any other options."

"So, do you really believe that we collared the wrong guy?" Attiq asked.

"Maybe," Jesse said softly. "It's a hard concept to compute, but maybe we did screw up."

~~~~~~~~~~

"He ran!" David Parrish complained to Sam Spade. "The stupid idiot ran, and that doesn't bode well for his long-term survival. Law enforcers, not to mention bounty hunters, can get pretty trigger happy and kill him on sight. What was he thinking?"

"Maybe he was thinking that he didn't want to face the death penalty or spend the rest of his life in prison for a crime he hadn't committed," Sam easily fielded that question.

"But it's only a matter of time until somebody spots him," David predicted, "then all bets are off as to how he'll wind up. I just hope it isn't in a body bag."

"Well, on the bright side, Michael's given us more time to investigate and find the evidence to clear him," the slick PI seemed inordinately blasé about the dangerous situation.

David suddenly looked at Sam and cocked an eyebrow. "Did you have anything to do with facilitating his escape, you old fool?"

"I certainly don't know why you would jump to that conclusion," Sam said incredulously. "Why do you always have such a suspicious nature?"

"When you answer a question with a question, it means that you're being evasive," David declared smugly. "You haven't done him any favors, you know. In fact, you have made it much worse."

"Everyone has an opinion these days," Sam mocked as he made his way to the door.

It wasn't until the former CIA operative was in his car and driving away that he placed a call on his burner phone. The conversation was cryptic, but both parties' innocent inferences spoke volumes.

"Hey there, Duff," Sam said cheerfully. "How's it going these days? I hope business is good, and I'll bet you're busy shipping out fragile merchandise to satisfied customers all the time. Tell me—have you got any handsomely crafted armoires currently in transit to an expectant customer?"

"As a matter of fact," the Italian manager of Symington and Son responded proudly, "we're doing exceptionally well in the import/export market. It must be due to the improving economy. Things are coming and going all the time, just as you thought. We actually sent a delicate package on its way yesterday to a secure home. Of course, it was meticulously wrapped and protected because of its valuable nature."

"That's good to know," Sam answered.

"We really need to keep in touch more often," the furtive old Mafia representative murmured before he disconnected.

Sam's next call went to another anonymous burner phone in San Francisco. It vibrated in the pocket of Defensive Attorney Lawrence Buchanan during a boring trial in which he was representing a client accused of car theft. He immediately asked the presiding judge for a five minute recess.

"Call of nature, Judge. Sorry about this. Must have been something bad that I ate," he explained with an embarrassed grimace.

The crusty magistrate sighed from his perch above the courtroom.

"Since it's almost the noon hour, let's take a break for lunch. And please, Mr. Buchanan, get yourself some Pepto Bismol before you return this afternoon!"

~~~~~~~~~

"What's the latest?" Lawrence asked from inside a stall in the empty men's room."

"Tell your sister all is well and to sit tight," Sam said tersely.

"Are you and your other friend still going to be working this on your end?" Michael's brother-in-law wanted to know.

"Yep, we're still on it!" Sam replied with a determined air. David didn't know it yet, but they both needed to put their noses to the proverbial grindstone once again. There was a lot more work to do. Sam began the process by sending a coded message on its way through the ether to a little fastidious hacker savant in London. The first order of business was a raft of red herrings.

Chapter Thirty-Eight

"Damn!" Detective Jesse Cormier complained in disgruntled exasperation. "Devereaux must be flying around the world on a magic carpet. The FBI notified us that there were reported sightings of him this past week in Caracas, Singapore, Berlin, and Sydney."

"Yeah, isn't that a real hoot," Attiq chortled. "Although it's tempting to try and see the world on somebody else's dime, I doubt any global travel vouchers that we submit to Metro are going to be approved."

"You know it!" Jesse agreed. "Most likely the US Marshals Service gets to go on those turkey hunts. We're just supposed to sit on our hands and let them hog all the glory if they ever do finally nab him. But, somehow, I don't see that happening anytime soon. I think Devereaux will stay underground unless something changes in the Abrams murder case."

"Now, Jesse," Attiq replied facetiously, "you know that our captain told us to stand down on any more investigating. As far as the department is concerned, this case is solved and closed up tight as a clam."

Jesse gave his partner a doleful look. "Uh huh, but we're not going to actually stand down, are we? Not when we have our doubts about the validity of the bust. I don't know about you, but I'm going to put in some effort on the down low. Maybe, if there is another doer out there, he'll think that the heat is off, and he'll become a bit complacent and sloppy. I'll wager he's probably congratulating himself right now on getting away with murder and letting someone else take the fall."

"Okay, so now the one big question remains—where do we start?" Attiq said with a sigh.

~~~~~~~~~

Attorney Manus Kirshner had a good idea where he could start probing. The shrewd lawyer had a lot of old friends from back in the day, and he was not above using those contacts to help his client. For the last several days, he had been diligently brainstorming with Sam and David for hours. Finally, they all agreed that they needed more dirt on the slain Senator to move ahead in their investigation. They needed to know who might have hated him enough to kill him. Ergo, tonight Manus was about to embark on a fact-finding mission.

Being a native Baltimorean born into substantial wealth, Manus had grown up in a cosseted little bubble in an era when young men and women of a certain strata were educated in small, elite, same-gender prep schools. The students wore uniforms—staid jackets and ties for the boys, and plaid skirts and blazers for the girls. It was all very conservative and genteel, and many long-lasting relationships were made that transcended the lengthening decades as well as the many miles of distance. The best friends that Manus had made when he was ten still exchanged Christmas cards as the milestone years of 40, 50, even 60 passed. Some of those comrades had settled locally while others were not that much farther away.

Tonight Mr. and Mrs. Manus Kirshner would be dining out with one such old acquaintance and his wife. The two couples had made long-overdue arrangements to meet on the outskirts of Washington, DC. Their choice of venue was the prestigious "Inn at Little Washington." The restaurant on the premises was five-star quality all the way as well as a perennial favorite with the Zagat and Michelin guidebooks.

Manus' friend, Stuart Woodworth, had aged well. Although now in his seventies, he still had a thick head of silver hair and looked to be just a few pounds over the weight that he carried during his younger salad days. He had none of the stooped-over posture of osteoporosis, and wore his dove grey three-piece suit and rep tie with an understated flair. Elyse, his wife of over fifty of those past years, was an elegant matron in her own right.

Perhaps a dedicated purpose in life had attributed to the graceful passage into the twilight of their years. Both people in this union never let any grass grow under their feet. There were no daytime serials or slow strolls through the park for them. They doggedly continued to be active and involved in their jobs and the swirling social life of the nation's capital.

Stuart held a lofty position in The Bureau of International Labor Affairs on Constitution Avenue in the District, and Elyse was a part-time preceptor, as well as a dedicated docent, at the Hirshhorn Museum on Independence Avenue. They were regulars at various social events that seemed to happen weekly, and being on Washington hostesses' "A List" kept them plugged in to just about everything that was happening in their corner of the world.

Dinner was a very elegant and pleasant affair. The service was impeccable, and the perfect main courses could only be described as gastronomic extravaganzas to tease and delight the palate. While the men were enjoying an after-dinner vintage port, their wives gracefully rose and made their way to the ladies room.

Stuart was now locking eyes with Manus and quirking a cynical little smile.

"This impromptu reunion was a fantastic idea," he began slowly, "but please don't try to kid a kidder, Manus. There's an ulterior motive behind this overture, and it isn't hard to figure out what that is. You could have just come right out and asked, you know. Our valued friendship warrants that cooperation."

Manus sighed. "You were always one step ahead of every-body, Stu, but couldn't you at least let me think that I was being slick and crafty."

"Oh, you're all of that and more, my friend," Woodworth assured him. "It's just that after living in this little town for decades, I've learned how to play the subterfuge game and to be a bit more suspicious and Machiavellian. That's a sad fact but, unfortunately, very true.

So, let's cut to the chase. What do you want to know about Jarod Abrams? I'm aware that you were representing Michael Devereaux before he took a powder. Now, I suppose that you are trying to find an alternate suspect for his father's murder. Well, old friend, that's a very long list. That piece of crap senator screwed a lot of people both literally and figuratively. Do you wish me to start chronologically or alphabetically?"

While Stu Woodworth expounded on a cornucopia of other congressmen, lobbyists, and private businessmen, his spouse was giving Manus' wife an earful while they sat in front of make-up mirrors in the powder room.

"I don't wish to sound crass," Elyse Woodworth whispered conspiratorially, "but Abrams was a horny hyena who would bang anything with a vagina. That bachelor pad of his was a real comfy little love nest where he had trysts by the dozen."

Then she began naming names—a lot of names!

Manus' wife listened closely to the sordid tale and looked appropriately shocked even though she already knew of his slimy reputation. Tonight, she was on her own fact-finding mission.

"Did his wife know?" she asked carefully.

"Of course, Sheila Abrams knew. She just pretended that she didn't," Elyse replied knowingly.

"She must have been mortified when she heard all of those ugly rumors," Mrs. Kirshner encouraged.

"Oh, I'm sure that she was, but what was she supposed to do?" Elyse asked pragmatically. "She had years invested in the marriage and had never attempted to create a life of her own outside of the home. It was as if Sheila was stuck in a time warp where her purpose was to keep the home fires burning and to support her man regardless of his peccadillos. Maybe she imagined herself to be Jackie Kennedy, regal and above it all. Back then, everybody knew handsome old Jack had a piece on the side from time to time, but Jackie kept her head held high and everyone adored her for her fortitude."

"I think that I'd castrate Manus if he ever strayed," his wife declared.

Elyse gave a decidedly unladylike snort. "Yeah, Stu and I are on the same page, so he's managed to hold onto his balls as well."

When the two bawdy women eventually left the bathroom a few moments later after their gossipy conversation, they again resumed a respectable and refined matronly air.

Chapter Thirty-Nine

Now it was a few days later back in Baltimore. Sam, David, Manus, and Ellis were spread out at a large conference table at the law office. Each had a small Chromebook in front of them and was deep into investigating all the innuendo that Stuart Woodworth and his wife had supplied after their cordial dinner reunion. There was quite a bit to delve into regarding the life and times of one very nefarious senator. The four men diligently made lists on yellow legal pads and tried to collate all the data into some semblance of order. In the end, they decided to do it from the very first instance, right up to the day that he was murdered.

Jarod Abrams had begun to feather his nest many years ago, just before he threw his hat into the senatorial ring. The first illustration of misconduct that they highlighted in the aspiring senator's march to Washington and political power was an instance of blatant gerrymandering in Northwest Baltimore County. "Gerrymandering" is a term which means that he underhandedly manipulated the boundaries of his electoral district to pretty much favor him in the election. Of course, it worked, and he was off and running.

Once ensconced in Congress, Abrams blazed a scorched earth trail in his wake. He routinely double-crossed lobbyists and other special interest groups by obtaining appropriations for other political coalitions who were in a better position to help him down the road. He routinely connived and lied to individuals, private companies, and even large corporations, causing some to eventually go belly-up because they had naively put all their eggs into Abrams' basket. He made empty promises to many others. There were enticing and lucrative defense contracts, and, for the besieged farming industry, much needed federal subsidies being dangled like a carrot in front of their noses. Most of the time, these things never happened.

Elyse Woodworth's gossip was juicy as well. Over the years, she claimed that Abrams had dozens of romantic liaisons. To catch his attention, you just had to be a pretty woman in a skirt. Most of his conquests were young and single, but others were married ladies and could have had very jealous husbands.

"Okay, it's a fact that Abrams was a horny stallion," Sam growled, "and his track record makes me feel just a tad inadequate. He certainly had a lot of stamina for a man his age. It looks like he was sometimes balancing three different affairs at the same time."

"He was handsome and powerful, and that's an aphrodisiac to some members of the fairer sex," David chimed in.

"And also a motive for payback," Sam agreed. "Maybe an enraged, cuckolded spouse of a defiled wife felt that he had to uphold his manhood. Even though such a fellow may not have actually done the deed himself, it certainly wouldn't be hard to hire somebody to do your dirty work for you. I've heard that people make anonymous connections like that on Craig's List quite often."

"Now the question remains—what are we supposed to do with all the suspicious dirt and the list of other possible suspects that we've managed to unearth?" David asked the room in general.

"Well, I can certainly take all of this information to the Washington authorities and plead my case," Ellis replied. "Maybe they'll reopen their investigation and begin looking at this with fresh eyes."

185

"Or maybe they'll just brush you off like a pain in the ass attorney trying to execute a Hail Mary play for his client," Sam said cynically.

When Ellis just shrugged, David spoke up.

"Maybe it's time that I inserted myself into this drama."

Sam lifted his eyebrows. "Now, why would you want to tip your hand at this late date, David? Nobody involved in the murder investigation knows of your relationship to Michael. You're our unknown ace in the hole if the time comes when we need one. You don't want exposure."

"It's not about what I want, or you want. It's about a debt that I need to repay," David answered. "Michael literally saved my life a few years ago, and now I've got to try to save his. If that means walking into the lion's den, then so be it."

"What's your plan?" Manus asked curiously.

"Instead of bringing this to the attention of the prosecuting attorney, I'm thinking that approaching the original detectives on the case may be a better option. Since I used to work in law enforcement, Cormier and Kabli may be more willing to hear me out and re-think the case from a different perspective."

"And they may tell you to stick your theories where the sun don't shine," Sam said dourly.

"There's always that possibility," David agreed, "but, it's like they say, nothing ventured, nothing gained. It won't hurt to try. I'll put all of our research on a flash drive and go to DC tomorrow."

~~~~~~~~~~

David headed for the nearby nation's capital on Thursday morning. For most of the day, he patiently staked out the detectives' precinct. Apparently, today was a paperwork day for the pair. He didn't see either of them leave until a little after 7 pm when they took one car and headed over to a little hole-in-the-wall sports bar. When David entered, he saw the two men perched on tall padded stools watching a Ravens game in progress.

The former FBI man strolled over and took a seat, leaving one empty chair between himself and the detectives who were nursing beers and popping pretzels and peanuts into their mouths.

David watched the Ravens/Steelers smash up for a few seconds before he remarked to his drinking companions.

"Man, Baltimore's taking a shellacking tonight. Joe Flacco still has a powerful arm, but without receivers like Todd Heap and defensive men like Ray Lewis, it's tough."

"You got that right!" Jesse Cormier agreed with a grimace. "I knew Baltimore was headed for a fall, but it really sucks when it's Ben Roethlisberger who's puttin' on the big hurt."

David extended his hand to Jesse and Attiq. "Name's David Parrish. Can I buy you guys another round?"

"If you're buying, we're not gonna say no," Attiq quipped. "Why don't you order yourself a burger on us. We're waiting on our own order. They're pretty decent here, and the fries are thick and greasy and guaranteed to clog your arteries good and proper."

For the next half hour, the men exchanged a lot of sports commentary until the game broke for halftime. At that point, the conversation turned more personal.

"So, tell me what you fellas do when you're not critiquing football plays?" David asked casually.

"We're actually Metro detectives working out of the homicide division," Attiq informed him.

"No shit!" David said incredulously. "I used to do my fair share of that myself back in Baltimore. I was with the local FBI for decades."

Suddenly, David perceived a shuttered expression appear on his new comrades' faces.

"Oh, come on, guys. Don't take that tidbit to heart. In my provincial little town, we played nice with the local cops. It was all about teamwork and getting the job done right. We shared info because we were all determined to administer justice, and nobody was a glory hound. I suppose it might be a bit different down here where everybody appears to have their own political agenda."

"That's an understatement," Jesse agreed.

"So, David, have you officially retired from the Bureau?" Attiq asked curiously.

"Yeah, I have," David enlightened him. "Now, I'm into a new career as an author. You know what they always say—write what you know—so my last two fictional books have been about government intrigues and conspiracy plots within its ranks."

Attiq suddenly snapped his fingers. "I thought your name sounded familiar. You're that new author who routinely causes quite a stir in Congress. I read your first novel when it came out. Now I know why you retired from the FBI. You're probably considered to be persona non grata."

"Yeah, I guess that I did rattle a few cages," David said as he shrugged his shoulders modestly.

"So, what brings you to Washington now?" Jesse asked. "Are you doing background for another blockbuster about corruption and murder?"

"Actually, I've already done the research on my newest project, but now I feel the need to confirm some pretty biased allegations from some of my sources," David explained. "You see, this new book isn't going to be fiction. It's going to be more like an exposé or a documentary about Senator Jarod

Abrams. Readers are really into that true crime stuff now, and they eat up every little fact that you feed them."

When the two detectives suddenly looked interested, David continued to bait the hook.

"Listen up, guys. I've mined the mother lode when it came to Abrams. According to all of my sources, he was a real son of a bitch, and most people said that it was about time that somebody did the world a favor by removing him from it. Almost all have their doubts that Michael Devereaux was responsible. In fact, some claimed that he would have had to stand in line to do the honors."

"That case is solved," Attiq said firmly. "In fact, we were the ones who closed it."

"Really?" David said innocently. "Then this is my lucky day because I'd like to run some stuff by you two before I confront anyone and come off sounding accusatory. I most certainly wouldn't want to be sued for libel after the novel is published. I mean, some of my sources had their own ideas of who the real killer was and the motive, and it sure wasn't about 'who's your Daddy.' A lot of their theories sounded plausible, and it started me having my own doubts."

"We're off the case," Jesse objected.

"Look, I'm not asking you to compromise a case that you've already closed," David insisted. "I would just like another professional opinion before I start writing this up. I certainly won't quote you or anything. As a matter of fact, I just happen to have a spare copy of my notes on a flash drive right here in my briefcase. I'd appreciate if you would take a look and lend a brother lawman a hand, fellas."

Chapter Forty

"So, they actually went for it!" Sam said admiringly. "Maybe, my friend, you could have another retirement career option as a con man. I've heard it said that creativity doesn't recognize advancing dotage."

David gave Sam a droll look and ignored the implied insult. "Now, it all comes down to how curious and determined the detectives are. They explained to me that any digging had to be done off book, so, most likely, this will take quite a while. How long can Michael stay safe and hidden?"

"Why are you asking me?" Sam demanded.

"Don't play dumb, Buddy," David growled. "I know you're up to your ears in his stupendous escape, and you probably know exactly where he is."

"You have to stop smoking that wacky tobacky, you idiot, because you're not making one iota of sense," Sam quipped in return.

~~~~~~~~~

David placed two inquiring phone calls to the Washington detectives during the following month. Jesse and Attiq were being cautious and only said that they were looking into certain things and quietly checking alibis. Well, that was a less than promising response. Michael still remained on the lam, and although the Marshals hadn't a clue of his whereabouts, that was small comfort to David.

The former FBI agent knew in his heart that the young man hadn't done the unthinkable, and a life on the run was neither a fair nor an emotionally palatable way for him to exist. He belonged back in San Francisco with his wife and family. David finally called Amy one evening to ask how she was holding up. The conversation was short and stilted, and certainly less than satisfying for David. Maybe he should have respected a worried wife's privacy.

However, the following month heralded some cautiously upbeat news. Sam had somehow gotten a message from a dependable foreign source urging him down a different, uncharted path. Professor Plum, bless his weird little heart, had finally come through for Michael.

"David, you've got to contact your good buddies in DC and put a bug in their ear," Sam prodded. "Tell them to go over the camera footage of Abrams' apartment building again. But, this time, tell them to expand their parameters in both directions. In other words, tell them to look at the much earlier as well as the much later hours of footage. Hopefully, if they go backward and forward far enough in time, they'll spot something that just may change the outcome of the whole friggin' ballgame."

"What should, or rather *who*, should they be looking for if they do that?" David wanted to know. "And, by the way, who passed along this tip?"

"If I told you that, I'd have to kill you," Sam replied just as he had before, and David wasn't convinced that he didn't mean it. Sam was a strange and shadowy character, and, more than likely, he hobnobbed with others of the same mold from a former clandestine life as a spy. Nonetheless, David would make a pact with the devil if it would help Michael.

When David made that fateful call to Cormier and Abli, he sensed that they were slowly being converted to believing that there could possibly be another culprit out there responsible for Abrams' murder. They swore to him that they would come into the precinct office on Sunday when their captain wasn't in house and sign out the camera reels from the evidence locker. They made no firm promises, but they said they'd give it the old college try.

~~~~~~~~~~

Meanwhile, Amy Devereaux remained in the sad house on Steiner Street in San Francisco and continued to worry. It seemed as if the FBI had given up on the dreary task of sitting at the outside curb. Nonetheless, she knew that she was still being watched whenever she went out. Likewise, she could still detect that faint telltale click on her phone indicating that someone was listening in on all her conversations. Let them record everything to their heart's content, she thought bitterly. I am not a stupid person, and neither is my husband. We can certainly hold our own in a deadly game of cat and mouse. Bring it on, fellas, but be prepared to lose!

Then one night, Amy found herself becoming engrossed in an evening television special. She had seen the blurbs for it the last couple of nights on a cable station. Mrs. Sheila Abrams, Senator Abrams' widow, had agreed to end her self-imposed silence regarding her husband's death and to be interviewed by a well-known and respected news anchorwoman. Amy had promised herself that she wouldn't watch it, but on the designated evening, she couldn't help herself and was drawn to the tv screen like a moth to a flame.

The chicly dressed and pristinely coiffed television persona sat stiffly erect with perfect posture in what appeared to be the Abrams' living room in Baltimore County. Sheila Abrams sat opposite her guest in a high-back Queen Anne chair. The grieving widow, years older than her nationally renowned interviewer, looked surprisingly composed and resolute. As

192

the cameras began to roll, the syndicated news maven quickly got the show on the road.

"Mrs. Abrams, I would like to thank you for agreeing to talk with me about the horrendous tragedy that has impacted your life and the lives of your sons. Doing this interview is a very brave thing to undertake, and I'm sure that the hearts of our viewers go out to you."

"Thank you, Georgina," Sheila Abrams replied in her well-modulated voice. "I have been a recluse for far too long, and I believe that it is time for me to come out of the shadows to set the record straight."

"Well, I'm sure that everyone will applaud your fortitude," the television persona said in her silky voice. "Now, Mrs. Abrams, it has been almost a year since your husband was brutally murdered and his killer was apprehended. How do you feel about the fact that Michael Devereaux escaped from federal custody before his scheduled trial four months ago? With that escape, he managed to elude justice, as well."

Sheila Abrams seemed to sit a little taller. "I think that you are jumping the gun and being quite judgmental by saying that, Georgina. Mr. Devereaux never had his day in court so he hasn't been found guilty of anything yet."

That seemed to throw the anchorwoman off her stride. Amy wondered if perhaps there had been a script and the Senator's wife wasn't following it.

"Mrs. Abrams, are you saying that you might have doubts about Mr. Devereaux's guilt," the interviewer asked with her eyebrows raised. There wasn't a corresponding wrinkle in her forehead thanks to Botox. "According to our sources, the Metro police had developed a strong case that they handed to the federal prosecutor on a silver platter. How could you possibly believe that your husband's illegitimate son didn't commit cold-blooded patricide? I certainly don't know your opinion of capital punishment, but to me, this egregious crime seems like it falls into that category."

"Of course, you are entitled to your own opinion," Sheila Abrams said patiently, "but I don't espouse the harsh Old Testament version of an eye for an eye. I believe there are always shades of grey that cloud any issue."

"Would you care to elaborate on that?" the interviewer urged, thinking that perhaps the network was going to get an unexpected scoop and the Nielsen ratings would soar.

Chapter Forty-One

Sheila Abrams squared her delicate shoulders and proceeded to accommodate the network executives and their dreams of glory.

"I've had long discussions with my two sons, and I have even spoken with the rabbi from my own congregation. I feel secure in the knowledge that I have their complete support. Thus, I have thought long and hard about what I'm about to say, and I have finally come to terms with what I believe is a necessary endeavor. It's definitely time to stop all the lurid rumor mongering and to set the record straight."

The anchorwoman started to interject a comment, but the Senator's wife held up a manicured hand to preclude the interruption.

"I would appreciate being afforded the courtesy of speaking without any distractions," she said primly, effectively shutting the moderator down.

"My generation," Mrs. Abrams began slowly, "was one in which family matters were kept personal. We espoused and valued discretion, and we certainly didn't air our dirty linen in public. In fact, we didn't ever speak of our problems outside of our homes. Of course, others knew of our secrets, but refrained from rubbing our noses in it. However, when Jarod decided to enter the public arena of politics, we were scrutinized even more closely, and there was a greater audience of prying eyes that feasted on every prurient detail.

So, in the interest of full disclosure, let's start with the irrefutable facts. As has come to light recently, my husband was a blatant womanizer. Apparently, that trait was something which started early in his life. He fathered a child when he was just eighteen years old and refused to acknowledge his responsibility to the underage girl that he impregnated or to her infant son, Michael Devereaux. I think that is a sin and unforgivable.

To be honest, I knew of Jarod's many affairs quite soon after our marriage, and, at first, I blamed myself. Apparently, I wasn't capable of satisfying his needs, so he went looking elsewhere. Those continuing hurtful acts eroded any self-esteem that I had. I foolishly tried to hold my head up and pretend to be an adoring and supportive wife through it all. Looking back on those days now, I'm sure everybody was snickering behind my back and thinking, 'poor, stupid Sheila.'

Well, poor, stupid Sheila wasn't clueless. I was really a coward. I never stood up to my husband. I never had the courage to speak my mind openly and demand that he stop his philandering for the sake of our marriage. However, that all changes right now. I am finally speaking up for myself. How sad that it takes a death to make another person want to restructure their own life as a different person—a better, stronger person.

I want to tell the awful truth of my marriage. The very first thing entails making everyone who is listening to this broadcast tonight aware that my husband wasn't a nice man. In truth, he was an evil person. I don't know if he ever loved me or even the two sons that we had together. He was an aloof and insensitive father, and a cruel husband who routinely demeaned me and undermined me at every turn. There were days when I hated him because he knew how to push the right buttons to make me feel worthless. Jarod had a knack for doing that to people.

Everyone has a breaking point when they're pushed to the edge beyond their endurance and they snap. Jarod liked being responsible for breaking people that way. So, if you were to ask me if I thought that was the reason that he was killed, I would tend to agree. However, I can't say, with any certainty, that his executioner was Michael Devereaux.

I have never met my husband's first offspring, and all that I know about him is what I have been told by the authorities. I have been made aware that he has a wife and four young children in San Francisco. My heart goes out to that family. Mrs. Devereaux has lost her husband, just as I have, and her children are probably missing their father as well. Even from the grave, Jarod has managed to ruin more lives, and that is very sad."

Having finally said her piece, the composed and valiant matron sat back in her chair and demurely folded her hands in her lap.

The moderator, however, looked wide-eyed and jubilant as she envisioned what was probably going to be the coup of her career. This interview would probably rival the one that a sad, depressed Princess Diana had given after her separation from Prince Charles. Viewers would lap it up.

Amy, watching from her sofa, looked shocked as well. This painful recitation was certainly not what she had expected to hear. Sheila Abrams had been quietly spectacular, managing to come across as rejected but also determinedly resolute to confess about her previous plight. It was obvious that it was a sort of catharsis, and she intended to turn her life around and begin living for herself. She didn't want pity. She wanted vindication for all the years of emotional abuse at the hands of her despicable husband.

Minutes after the presentation had ended, the burner phone that Amy always kept in her pocket vibrated.

"Did you watch it?" Sam asked without any preamble.

"Yes, I did," Amy answered, "and it certainly wasn't what I expected."

"Yeah, the lady sure orchestrated her own version of shock and awe," Sam agreed.

Sam was never one for small talk, so he then began making Amy aware of the latest developments in their investigation. Now, Amy knew what she had to do. She'd pack an overnight bag in the morning and be on the next plane headed East.

Chapter Forty-Two

"You don't have to do this, you know," Sam said softly to Michael's wife as they sat idling in the driveway of a Tudor mansion in Baltimore's Greenspring Valley.

"Yes, I do. I just can't sit around and wait on the sidelines. I need to help save my husband," the young woman responded emphatically.

"I'll be right here the whole time," Sam promised.

Amy just gave him a little smile and exited the Hummer. She had dressed carefully for this encounter today in classic black slacks and a crisp white blouse. The heels of her black flats made clicking sounds as she resolutely walked up the flagstone path to the carved oak front door. She expected to be met by a maid or housekeeper, but it was Sheila Abrams, herself, who answered the melodious chimes.

The two women who shared a strange bond stared at each other for a brief second, and Amy wondered if the elegant matron would close the door in her face. However, Sheila Abrams surprised her by graciously inviting her unexpected visitor into a marble-tiled foyer illuminated by a massive crystal chandelier hanging from a vaulted ceiling.

"I supposed we were destined to meet at some point in time," the older woman murmured softly.

Amy nodded. "Yes, I think we were."

Sheila Abrams beckoned for her guest to follow as she led the way through spacious rooms with rich Oriental rugs on the hardwood floors, cream colored sofas facing marble fireplaces, and conservative oil paintings displayed on the walls. Everything was precisely arranged and immaculate.

However, Amy thought that the surroundings lacked a warm, comfortable ambience. Everything looked staged as if an interior decorator had temporarily stepped away from the scene because a photo shoot by "House Beautiful" was about to take place. To Amy's eye, the large house didn't seem lived-in at all. Instead, it looked cold and sterile and empty.

Eventually, the two women made their way to a smaller room at the rear of the home. There was a different vibe here, and it was peaceful and tranquil. Amy surmised that this was Sheila's sanctuary. It was definitely feminine in nature. The walls were painted a soft aqua, and quilted cornices in a floral pattern bracketed the room's two windows. There was a delicate writing desk inlaid with mother of pearl at one end. A brocade settee and a chaise lounge took up space at the other. The latter had a soft rumpled afghan thrown across its wide cushion, but Amy could see a needlepoint work in progress peeking out.

Her hostess waved Amy towards the settee, but, instead, Michael's wife walked over to stare at the wall behind the small escritoire. The entire expanse was covered with framed pictures of two boys as he progressed through the years from childhood to becoming young adults.

"Did you know that I first met my husband almost twenty years ago. He wasn't much older than your sons back then," Amy said softly. "Your eldest boy could pass for his clone. And the pictures of them when they were younger, well, they're my own twins' doubles."

"I've been told that you have sons as well," the Senator's widow murmured.

"Yes, three sons and a daughter, and they all look like their father. Apparently, the Abrams' genes manifest themselves over and over." Amy answered.

"I would have liked a daughter someday, but it just wasn't meant to be," Sheila said almost wistfully. "Truthfully, Jarod was content with sons because he saw them as a legacy to carry on his name. He never was involved in their upbringing, so I gladly took up the slack and my children became my world. The boys and I were, and still are, extremely close.

However, that didn't stop Jarod from stepping in to map out their futures to his liking. Their wishes never mattered. He claimed that Jason and Justin had a destiny to fulfill, so they were relegated to being part of the facade that my husband had built. They were a means to an end for him—tools to be used—just like everything else in his life."

Amy had no response for that, so she remained mute as Sheila Abrams perched on the small settee.

"Is your husband a good father?" the bitter woman finally asked.

"Yes, Michael is a loving and kind father," Amy answered as she sat beside Mrs. Abrams.

The young woman than reached inside her purse to extract a 5 x 7 photograph. It was a candid moment that Amy had managed to capture last summer when the entire family was enjoying a sailing outing on Michael's sloop. The sun had been shining and the wind was carelessly ruffling the hair of the five people in the picture. Michael looked tanned and handsome, his wide smile causing little crinkles to form at the corners of his blue eyes. Philip had his arm around his father and appeared to be laughing, while Ella was simply looking up at her Dad with a look of pure adoration. The twins were hanging on Michael's legs and mugging for the camera with crossed eyes and tongues lolling.

"Michael is a wonderful husband as well," Amy continued. "He always says that the kids and I are his entire world, and he really means that."

"You look like such a very happy family," Sheila whispered as she studied the picture.

"We are, or at least we were, until this tragedy unfolded," Amy said sadly.

There was silence for almost a full minute until it was Sheila Abrams who felt the need to break it.

"A mother is like a lioness or a mama bear," she began. "She'll do whatever is necessary to protect her young. I'm sure that you would agree, Mrs. Devereaux."

Amy merely nodded her head mutely and waited for Sheila Abrams to continue.

"Somehow, things got turned around in my family," the woman said sadly. "The boys thought that they had to protect *me*. When the first emails arrived from the woman who claimed to be your husband, Jason and Justin confronted their father before ever bringing it to my attention. Jarod denied everything, of course, but the boys knew better. They had grown up in the same house with their father, and they had heard the gossip from kids at school who had heard it from their parents. It was all so sordid and ugly.

Of course, I did nothing about it over the years, so it's my fault that my sons perceived me as weak and vulnerable. I should have developed a spine and been a better role model for them.

Eventually, they did come to me when the emails evolved into blatant blackmail. I wanted to protect Jason and Justin from the fallout stemming from an embarrassing secret in their father's past. Jason was graduating law school and on the cusp of being hired by a prestigious New York firm. A scandal like that would ruin his future as well as his younger brother's when he ultimately ventured out into the career field.

So, in desperation, I began to acquire the money that was necessary to meet the many blackmail demands. Jarod always handled the finances, so I had no access to our accounts. I had only one other recourse. I began to pawn things for cash, and I would send it to the designated post office box. At first, it was my grandmother's collection of Royal Derby china, then her antique pearls, and an exquisite emerald ring. When the amount of hush money kept escalating, I pawned my own engagement ring. When I was out of items that would go unnoticed by my husband, I became frantic."

"What did you finally do?" Amy prodded softly, noting the haunted look in her hostess' eyes. There was an ominous silence before the older woman took a deep breath and responded. It looked as if she had come to a crossroads and had made some kind of decision about which direction she would take.

"I went to Jarod's apartment in Washington," she began in a flat monotone. "I knew where it was, and I even had a key. I had secretly made a copy when Jarod was laid up in bed here at home with the flu last year. I wanted to confront him with the devastation that he had caused with his irresponsible behavior a lifetime ago. I wanted to beg him to somehow fix this thing. At the time, I thought that maybe he could contact his illegitimate son and make amends. If that didn't work, I thought he should make a public statement along with an ardent mea culpa. Maybe, if he got out in front of this error in judgment, it would be more palatable for his constituents and they might forgive him."

"But it didn't go as planned, did it?" Amy said softly.

"No, it didn't," Sheila Abrams answered softly without meeting Amy's eyes. "I drove to DC early in the afternoon because I'm very nervous being on the Capitol Beltway during rush hour. I think that I actually arrived around 4 pm, long before Jarod got home. I let myself into the apartment and was shocked to find copies of those horrible emails sitting out in

203

the open right on the kitchen counter. I knew they hadn't been forwarded to him by our boys, so he must have gotten them in some underhanded way.

However, it also meant that even though Jarod already knew what was happening, he had done nothing to put an end to it. I waited and waited, and got angrier by the minute. When Jarod came home much later that evening, we had a confrontation that quickly escalated. I didn't tell him about the payments that I had been making, but he was angry just the same. He was livid because I had the audacity to invade his personal space, and he made it clear that I wasn't welcome.

We were in the kitchen having quite a row when someone rang the door buzzer. Jarod shushed me and told me to go into the bedroom and keep my mouth shut. I thought that maybe one of his girlfriends had come calling, but then I heard a man's voice and I listened very closely. Of course, that man was your husband, Mrs. Devereaux. I figured that out from their conversation. It didn't take long before it was over because it was obvious that the great and masterful Jarod Abrams had been played for a fool and had even taken a punch from your husband for good measure.

When I returned to the kitchen, I actually taunted Jarod about that fact and that made him furious. He called me a stupid cow and a lot of other even more vicious names. Suddenly, he had a liquor bottle in his hand and was hurling it across the kitchen at my head. It smashed against the cabinets, with glass and Scotch flying everywhere. I slipped in the sticky liquid and went down, but then I saw Jarod come around the kitchen island and he looked insane. God help me, I grabbed hold of the bottleneck lying beside me on the floor and lunged at him."

An eerie, faraway expression suddenly took over the older woman's face.

"It didn't take very long for Jarod to die. At first, he looked puzzled, like he couldn't quite grasp what was happening. But then those beautiful blues eyes began to look frantic, and he started making this weird gurgling sound. I just sat on the floor beside him in shock. It felt as if I was outside of my body watching everything take place in slow motion.

I think that I must had blacked out at some point. Hours later, I slowly became aware. At first, I thought that I was at home having a nightmare, but when I looked around and saw Jarod lying in a pool of blood, I realized the horrible dream had been real. It was too late to help my husband, but I had to protect my sons. They were going to need me more than ever now. They had lost their father, and they just couldn't lose their mother, as well.

So, I cleaned up any evidence of my being in the apartment and tried to get rid of the glass shards and those damn email copies. I swear to you, I never thought that the police would tie your husband to Jarod's death."

Amy leveled her gaze on Sheila Abrams. "They tied him to your husband's *murder*, Sheila, and now an innocent husband and father is in jeopardy of losing his life or his freedom. Thanks to his father, Michael was thrown to the wolves when he was born, and now you're doing the same thing to him again. Please come forward and tell the truth for everyone's sake," Amy pleaded.

"I just can't," Sheila said softly. "I'm sorry, but you have to understand that I just can't do that," she repeated.

"I'm sorry, too," Amy murmured as she rose from the settee and left a room that was so full of pathos. She then quickly found the front entrance and let herself out of the soulless, unfeeling house.

Chapter Forty-Three

Amy opened the door to Sam's car, nodded her head slightly, then let out her breath in one long whoosh. The PI patted her affectionately on the shoulder and drove slowly down the cul du sac to where a black Chevy Suburban was parked at the curb. Sam stepped out and approached the vehicle as the window powered down. The three occupants, David Parrish, Jesse Cormier, and Attiq Kabli, came into view.

"Did you get all that?" Sam asked the trio.

"Yep, loud and clear, although it really wasn't what we had hoped to get in our hot little hands," Attiq said morosely as he removed the headphones and then pointed to the recording equipment beside him.

"Well, you play the hand that you're dealt," Sam replied.

When Sam rejoined Amy, the young woman had her hand under her blouse discretely pulling away the surgical tape that held the tiny microphone in place on her chest.

"Are you okay, Sweetheart?" he asked solicitously.

Amy didn't answer him directly. Instead, she murmured soft words while staring through the windshield at absolutely nothing.

"It was like she said. She's a mother, and a mother has to protect her children any way that she can."

~~~~~~~~~~

Jesse drove towards Baltimore City where they were next going to drop David off at his downtown apartment. The DC detectives had allowed him to accompany them on this off-book caper as a professional courtesy. They felt that they owed him because he had been the one to point them in the direction of the smoking gun.

"Are you going to write about this after the dust settles, *Mr. Best Selling Author*?" Attiq asked.

David was thoughtful. "I guess that really depends on how you play it."

"How *are* we going to play this?" Jesse asked his partner as they later swung around the Interstate 95 ramp back towards the nation's capital.

"Any way that we do proceed will definitely suck," Attiq grimaced, "but you know that we have to present all the facts and do it right."

"If we go with just the confession, Mrs. Abrams might not make out too bad," Jesse mused. "After that heart-wrenching television interview, she has a lot of public sympathy behind her. Maybe some lenient judge will consider the extenuating circumstances and send her to a Club Fed for a year or two. Martha Stewart made the most of the five months she was sent to the one in West Virginia. I heard she gave cooking lessons. Maybe Sheila Abrams can give lectures on how to stop being a victim."

Attiq sighed. "When we write up our report and forward it to the state troopers in the proper jurisdiction, we have to add everything that we have to cover our own asses. That includes the earlier footage from those condo cameras. We just can't ignore what we saw and leave it out."

"Yeah, I know you're right. It seems that any way that we go means destroying lives," Jesse mused.

Attiq gave his partner a sidelong glance. "Jess, you've met Devereaux's wife. Don't you think that we've already messed up that lady's life as well as the lives of her kids and her husband? As hard as it is, it's time to make this right."

By the time that the two conflicted partners reached their precinct office, they were in agreement. They immediately took their captain into their confidence, owned up to their unsanctioned investigation, and played the taped confession. The miscreants even sheepishly added that they had prudently obtained a proper wiretap warrant beforehand from a crusty old federal judge in Baltimore who was bordering on senility.

Their superior wasn't happy about being kept out of the loop, but he gave the two mavericks carte blanche to officially reopen the Abrams homicide case. That included official permission to sign out the camera footage that they had already gone over a second time from the evidence locker.

Attiq set everything up in a conference room with a pull-down whiteboard and was all prepared to rerun the late afternoon and the next morning's early footage on those tapes. However, the strange difficulties were just beginning. When he pushed 'play,' every frame of the video was now just white snow with irritating noisy static. Jesse stepped in and ran the tape forward and backward, again and again, but distinct pixels were no longer present. Instead, they had coalesced into gray and white lines that streaked across the screen.

"Son of a bitch!" Jesse murmured.

"That's not exactly what you claimed to have seen when you snooped a second time, is it?" their captain said with a degree of sarcasm.

No, it really wasn't. What the detectives saw less than forty-eight hours ago was an entirely different movie. Instead of Sheila Abrams slinking into her husband's apartment at 4 o'clock on the afternoon of that fateful day, it had been her sons doing the clandestine entering. Jason had taken a key from his pocket and quickly let himself and his brother in. However, the two boys did not exit that apartment until 2 o'clock the following morning when the footage very clearly showed the apartment door inch open and a dark head cautiously peer out into the hall. Justin left first carrying a plastic sack, and Jason followed on his heels. The older brother had gently pulled the door closed behind him and then tugged down the sleeve of his Henley shirt to wipe his prints from the door knob.

The precinct captain sighed. "Look, guys, you have the lady's confession. If she chooses to be the sacrificial lamb in all this, then who are we to contradict her? Finish your report and call the proper people up in Baltimore to make the arrest. You can then go and collect the Senator's wife after that goes down."

Once back at their desks, Jesse asked, "Do you think she knew?"

"Of course, she knew," Attiq said irritably. "She had the details all down pat. Her helpful little boys had probably run home to tell Mommy all about it that same morning. She just tweaked the story a bit in her own version to make herself look pitiful and sympathetic. She probably sent her sons back to college immediately so that they were out of sight. We looked into them superficially, but they alibied each other and were supposedly several hundred miles away at the time. I guess by then, we had tunnel vision because we were focused on Michael Devereaux. It was a classic clusterfuck on our part."

"We'll probably never know which one of them actually did it, will we?" Jesse said.

"Not likely," Attiq agreed, "but it doesn't really matter in the long run, I guess."

Chapter Forty-Four

Of course, the media was having orgasmic spasms over this latest twist in the murder of Senator Jarod Abrams. The man's wife was now in custody, and her sad, forlorn picture was featured above the fold in all the remaining newspapers distributed across the nation. Most folks got the low down from their nightly news anchors or the Internet. By whichever route the scandalous and shocking information was relayed, it made Sheila Abrams the talk of the town.

Not surprisingly, most people, especially women, seemed sympathetic, and she was receiving daily letters of hopeful encouragement. She had also retained formidable counsel—a snarling Pit Bull of an attorney known for his ardent crusade to champion abused women who finally fought back against their oppressors. Sheila used the equity in her Tudor mansion to retain his services as well as to post her bail. She had surrendered her passport and was now again holed up in the Baltimore countryside, although this time she had an ankle monitor in place. Telephoto pictures captured by lurking paparazzi occasionally caught sight of her two sons visiting on weekends.

In the meantime, Manus Kirshner and Ellis Faraday had been extremely focused and busy. They had worked diligently to submit the proper paperwork to exonerate their client of all charges. Everything was sewn up tight in the stack of legal papers in their arsenal. Now, Michael just had to magically appear out of thin air so that he could sign them and go back to his quiet life before this debacle had occurred. Easy-peasy—

well, not really. No one seemed to know where the man was or where he had been for months.

~~~~~~~~~~

David Parrish was agitated. "C'mon, Sam, you must know where he is!"

"It's like I've told you a million times before, I haven't kept track of him!" the PI answered sharply.

"And just like I told you a million times before, I don't believe you!" David retaliated.

"You know, Mr. Ex-FBI man, you're really getting on my last nerve," Sam snarled. "You Fed guys are all alike with your lack of trust issues. Maybe I need a vacation from all this suspicion and these never-ending accusations."

"Good—go!" David urged. "And when you come back from wherever, make sure to bring Michael back with you!"

Sam quickly made tracks for the door, then stopped before actually leaving.

"Are you going to be writing a no-holds barred book about this Abrams thing after its all over and Sheila Abrams is sentenced," he asked curiously.

"Dunno," David answered honestly. "Probably not," he finally added. "I guess I tend to like happy endings, and this story certainly doesn't have any elements of that. Everyone got hurt in the process before it ended with a whimper instead of a bang."

"Leaving it be is probably for the best," Sam said sagely as he really started through the door this time. "That's what Michael would probably say."

~~~~~~~~~~

A cattle ranch situated in a bucolic Wyoming valley had the perfect vantage point to see for miles in all directions. The dust that Sam's car had kicked up on the ribbon of road that wound its way at the foot of the Grand Teton mountains alerted the occupants in the simple log structure on the property. Although only a handful of people knew it, Michael Devereaux had owned this spread for years. His crusty, old foreman, as well as his brother-in-law, were waiting on the porch of the main house when Sam cruised to a stop.

"We were wondering when you were going to show up," Lawrence Buchanan said as he extended his hand to Sam. It was the first time that the two men had actually met in person.

"Well, I stalled as long as I could to give Michael and his family some private, quality time before the circus begins," Sam said. "By the way, where is the ex-fugitive?"

"He rode out this morning to check on the herd in the north pasture," the foreman answered. "Philip and Ella went with him. Amy is with the twins down by the creek. The young ones are trying to catch tadpoles."

"Well, now that they've enjoyed their happy little reunion, Michael has to go back East again to finally make this right," Lawrence informed Sam pragmatically. "I'm going with him when he decides to make that move. However, I personally think that the sooner we get this done, the sooner everyone can get back to normal, or at least some semblance of whatever 'normal' is in the Devereaux world."

"I've known Michael since he was a kid," Sam said wisely. "He's strong and resilient so he'll bounce back, and so will Amy and the kids. They're all tough in their own way, so they'll get through it and come out the other side just fine."

"I'm not going to argue that point," Lawrence agreed.

~~~~~~~~~~

Later that night found Michael and Sam seated, side-by-side, on the front porch rockers. Each had a copious quantity of Jack Daniels in the glasses in their hands. The air was peaceful. The cicadas hummed, and it was comforting. The occasional hoot from a night owl was the only thing that interrupted the tranquility.

"I don't know how I can ever begin to thank you enough," Michael began, "and that goes for David, Duff, Manus, and Ellis as well. I don't feel as if I deserve that kind of loyalty."

"Don't be an idiot, Michael," Sam growled. "Just keep your mouth shut so that you don't wind up embarrassing yourself any more than you already have by adding another word to that stupid statement!"

"Well, I've already put it out there, so there's no taking it back," the younger man said stubbornly.

Sam snorted. "You always were willful and obstinate, even as a cheeky, wet-behind-the-ears kid. It's a wonder that Philip Symington and I managed to survive those early days with any hair left on our heads."

"I wasn't that bad," Michael objected.

Sam raised his eyebrows and gave Michael a level look. Then his expression softened as he went off on a tangent.

"It was such a freaky thing that happened to that video camera footage from Abrams' apartment building," he said thoughtfully. "Somehow, even though safely locked away in an evidence room in a police station, those reels managed to get erased or corrupted or something. How do you suppose that happened?"

"That is puzzling," Michael agreed. "I guess maybe it could have resulted from some kind of demagnetizing, like how a programmed key card for a particular hotel room suddenly stops working if you keep it too close to your cell phone. I also think that I read somewhere that a heavy duty magnet may do that if it's in close proximity for a short time."

"I guess that's as good of an explanation as any," Sam said with a smile.

"Yep. Works for me!" Michael agreed.

Epilogue

Six months later, Jason Abrams peered out of the peephole in the apartment that he shared with his brother in New Haven. He wasn't sure if he should open the door. The man probably wouldn't give up and just go away, so finally he summoned the courage to confront the person who stood before him. Justin was now at his brother's shoulder and equally nervous and confused.

"Can we talk for a few minutes?" Michael asked softly.

Jason just nodded his head mutely and stepped aside as his half-brother, who looked so much like their father, entered. Michael seemed relieved, and he actually gave them a little smile.

"I know this is really awkward for all of us, but I really wanted to see you," he began. "There are some things that I need to say, and putting it off isn't going to cut it for me."

"Okay," Jason said cautiously. "Justin and I are listening."

"I'm really sorry about your mother," Michael began. "She deserved a better life."

"Well, from what we were told, so did you," Justin said charitably.

"Yeah, well my beginnings weren't great, but they didn't ultimately define who I became. That was all on me," Michael explained, "and I'm certainly not proud of some of the stuff that I did along the way."

Now both Abrams brothers were looking down at their shoes instead of staring at their visitor, but Michael forged ahead anyway.

"We all do some things that we thought we would never be capable of doing. I know I have, and my rash actions continue to haunt me. But, in time, you try to do your penance in little ways to atone for your sins. It gets easier as you try to balance the scales. Some days, I forget that part of me and I'm happy. Hopefully, in time, you'll get to that place as well."

Both Jason and Justin looked leery. How much did this man really know?

Michael read their expressions and added, "I guess what I'm trying to say is that it will begin to fade as time passes, especially if you allow yourselves to move on in a positive direction."

"We can't move on yet. Mom is still incarcerated, and she'll need us when they finally let her leave that place," Justin said decisively.

"I was made aware that she was given a two-year sentence for the actions that she claimed were hers," Michael said carefully. "It's a long time, but not a lifetime. She'll probably be released early, and when that time comes, you both can help her to reinvent her life."

"Like you did?" Jason said it almost as a challenge.

"Yeah, like I did," Michael surprised him by agreeing.

"Finding your hidden strengths and nurturing them is a good thing, guys," he advised. "You can help your mother to discover hers, maybe not here, but somewhere else. It's a big wide world out there, and she can leave the bad memories behind once and for all. My family and I live in San Francisco and it's a great town. You'd always be welcome in my home if you decided to visit."

"You'd really want us around?" Justin sounded suspicious.

"You're my brothers, so, yeah, I *would* like that," Michael said honestly. "Even though we all came from the same father, none of us *are* him. We all need to remember that."

Finally, Michael put his hands in his pockets and shrugged his shoulders.

"That's what I came to say, and now that I've said it, I'll be on my way."

"Do you want to stay for awhile and maybe have a beer?" Jason suddenly asked.

Michael smiled softly, "It's too soon for that, but I'm hoping that perhaps, in time, it will seem more natural for you say something along those lines. That's when I'll take you up on the offer."

A sneak peek at the next book in the "Value" series that includes:

"A Person of Value"
"A Valuable Life"
"A Valuable Lesson"
"The Value of Everything and Nothing."

The upcoming 5ᵗʰ book details a series of threats to the wellbeing of all the characters that you now know quite intimately. It should hit Amazon in the late spring.

"Face Value"

The intruder was clad in dark clothes—black pants, black shirt, and a bulky black hoodie that served to obscure a face from the prying eyes of the security cameras mounted on the walls of the darkened museum. There was only an occasional anemic illumination from exit sign beacons which cast eerie shadows on the dim walls. Undoubtedly, a silent alarm had already been triggered, so there was just a small window of time to get the job done. This stealthy shadow had a simple stepladder in hand which was a necessary tool needed for the task. There was just one more implement that was required — a finely-honed boxcutter. Carefully climbing two steps, the determined entity set about the objective of this mission. In the blink of an eye, the face of the woman depicted in the valuable oil painting hanging on the wall was quickly slashed to ribbons with fevered intensity. The defacer—and wasn't that a fucking oxymoron—studied tonight's handiwork. There was no denying that it had felt good to obliterate those harsh, judgmental eyes. It helped to quell the turbulence, at least for a time. But maybe it just wasn't enough anymore to settle the swirling unrest of the mind.

www.ingramcontent.com/pod-product-compliance
Lightning Source LLC
Chambersburg PA
CBHW020613180626
46810CB00007B/2752